Agnes May Gleason

WALSENBURG, COLORADO, 1933

---

by Kathleen Duey

Aladdin Paperbacks

For Richard
For Ever

First Aladdin Paperbacks edition October 1998

Aladdin Paperbacks
An imprint of Simon & Schuster
Children's Publishing Division
1230 Avenue of the Americas
New York, NY 10020

Library of Congress Cataloging-in-Publication Data
Duey, Kathleen.
Agnes May Gleason, Walsenburg, Colorado, 1933 / by Kathleen Duey.
— 1st Aladdin Paperbacks ed.
p.   cm. — (American diaries ; #11)
Summary: In 1933, when her father's foot injury makes it impossible
for him to do farm work for a while, thirteen-year-old Agnes steps
in, proving herself and revealing her understanding of him.
ISBN 0-689-82329-0 (pbk.)
[1. Fathers—Fiction. 2. Farm life—Fiction. 3. Depressions—
1929—Fiction.]
I. Title. II. Series.
PZ7.D8694Ag   1998   98-30243
[Fic]—dc21
CIP   AC

Tuesday, June 6, 1933, Walsenburg, Colorado

And here I am again, hiding behind the hay wagon so Daddy can't see me and make me come help him move the old lumber pile!! I just want half an hour to myself . . .

Ralph has been gone two whole months, today. I don't know whether I am worried about him anymore, or just angry at him. First milking takes so long without his help that Daddy has had to leave late for deliveries almost every morning. And he has been hiring Mr. Thomas to help this past week—I can't carry milk crates anywhere near fast enough to please Daddy. He scolded me along the whole way the last time I went.

Mr. Thomas works for almost nothing since he is too old to get another job, but it's still money we could use for something else if Ralph hadn't left. I can't think about him without getting all steamed up. He will turn eighteen this week—wherever he is. The note he left Mama said he would send us money when he got a job. She thinks he went to the mines, but Daddy says he probably ran off to California or somewhere crazy like that, dreaming big about finding some way out of the hard times. Daddy says there isn't a way out—not for the common man, anyway. Last night, Daddy said Ralph is irresponsible and had best never come back, that if he does, he'll catch heck. That made Mama cry. They argue about Ralph a fair amount now.

I don't think he went to the mines. I wouldn't. I bet he never even applied with Colorado Iron and Fuel or the Walsen mine. The idea of going down in those black tunnels makes me shiver. I hate the sound the tipples make, too. It's like a landslide when the coal and rock fall to the ground. But I hope he hasn't gone to California. Daddy told me most of the boys that go looking for work like that wind up cold, hungry bums.

Last night I could hear Charles crying again. He's still not used to Ralph being gone and he gets scared in the dark. Daddy forbade him to turn on his light at night anymore—he says it costs too much and that Charles needs to grow up a little. Charles is only seven, but he's so serious he already seems older. Mary was fast asleep through the whole thing last night, even Daddy clomping down the hallway to tell Charles to get to sleep.

Mary is getting pretty, with a pixie mouth and nose. Her hair gets darker and heavier all the time. The rest of her still looks like a colt, all legs and knees and elbows, and her teeth seem too big for her, but

Mama says she will be a beauty and I think she is right. Not me. Not ever. Mary is only ten and I am almost thirteen and more boys look at her than at me.

Daddy is hammering at something now—probably breaking apart some of the old lumber—or maybe fixing the broken stanchion before evening milking. Mama says he works too hard. I know he is worried about losing the dairy to the bankers. He says the banks up in Denver and Pueblo are calling in loans on farmers right and left. On the radio news last night we heard about terrible things happening in Ohio—farmers getting into fights with marshals. It's the same old argument about the tuberculosis testing.

None of the dairymen here think the tests are accurate. Mr. Ugolini says they just kill the cows that react to the test and sell the meat anyway—then pay the farmer a low price for the cow. Who does that protect? He said at this rate, every farmer in this country will be bankrupt before long.

Money! Cows! Is that all I ever think about? I wonder what Ralph is thinking about right now. He has made everything so much harder for us all. I wonder if he ever feels bad about that—or if he ever even thinks about it at all.

In his last fireside chat, President Roosevelt said we will all come through these hard times if we work and help each other. I don't know. Mama hasn't had a new dress in two years—it seems like we never have the extra two or three dollars to spend. She makes flour-sack dresses for me and Mary. The boys wear made-over shirts of Daddy's. I wonder if Ralph will have better clothes to wear wherever he's gone. I just wish he hadn't gone anywhere. All of us have more chores now, to make up his work.

I have lost three of my bob-pins. I can't imagine how. I've had the same nine hairpins for nearly three years and haven't lost even one. I know Mama will never let me buy more—she disapproves so of my pin curls and bobbed hair. Daddy and Mama are so backward! Bobbed hair has been in style in the magazines for my whole life, I think. Aunt Mollie up in Denver has short hair and she's old. Sometimes I wish I had been born in Denver or Chicago or St. Louis—somewhere big and bustling with crowds of people.

Mary and Charles and I got to go into town yesterday and in Star's drug we wanted to get a soda, but Daddy said he didn't have three spare nickels—so we just had to stand there. I asked him about a puppy again. Daddy won't let me get a pup, even though old Scotty died nearly a year ago—he says we can't afford to give scraps to a dog when we can use whatever comes out of the kitchen and the cream separator to fatten pigs.

I will be so glad when these hard times are over. Daddy says President Roosevelt is a smart man and a strong-willed man and that if anyone can fix all this unemployment and bad times, it's him. Mama says Mrs. Roosevelt is a good-hearted woman who wants to help people all she can. So maybe they will figure out how to do it. I hope so. Ralph told me once that he could remember when we weren't very much worried about money. I sure can't.

CHAPTER ONE

Agnes shifted, loose hay prickling at her skin as she switched positions, straightening one leg, tucking the other beneath her. She sighed. It seemed like all she ever thought about was money—or the lack of it. Mama said there would be no money for school clothes again. That meant more flour-sack dresses for her and Mary, more cut down church-donation shirts and trousers for Charles. And probably no new shoes for anybody.

Agnes inhaled the sweet scent of the stacked hay and put her feet up on the rear wheel of the old flatbed hay wagon. The buggy whip stuck up from its holder at a sharp angle, and she stared at it absently, then looked past it to a flock of mallard ducks flying in a V toward Mrs. Otto's pond.

Agnes could smell the sage blooming on the gentle slope below the alfalfa pasture. She leaned back against the haystack for a moment and closed her eyes, letting the afternoon sun warm her face. Summer was about here. If she wasn't careful, her skin would turn as dark as old tea and Mama would scold and fuss and make her use vinegar and lemon to bleach it out again.

Agnes put the cover on her fountain pen, then lay it and her homemade diary carefully on the clean hay beside her. The rose-print fabric she had used for the cover had been cut from an old dress of Mama's that finally wore out completely. Agnes loved it. Someday, if she ever had a house of her own, she wanted wallpaper just like it.

Peering beneath the wagon, through the spokes of the wheels, she looked across the pasture at the house. This far away, it seemed small, like a square white dollhouse, pretty and perfect, with a twist of dark green and soft pink—Mama's tea rose—twining up a trellis beside the porch stairs. The line of pinions looked soft and blurred, like a watercolor painting.

The storybook effect was ruined instantly as she pictured the rusted-out plowshares and the old seeder leaning against the far side of the barn. They were rimmed with weeds, turning into heaps of papery, corroded iron that peeled off like tree bark. And the fence along the front by Elder Street was falling down because Daddy had no time nor the money to hire a hand to help with the work.

The delivery truck was hidden from sight by the house, but Agnes could imagine the painting of a cow framed by viney borders and yellow buttercups that stretched across its doors. Daddy had built a special rack in the back, sized to fit the bed of the truck perfectly, dividing it up into slots the exact dimensions of a crate of twelve, one-quart milk bottles. Agnes remembered it clearly. Ralph had helped Daddy build it. She had chased Charles and Mary around the yard, keeping them out of the way. Charles had wound up poking at the dirt with a long stick he'd found. Mary had climbed the smallest pinion so she could watch what Daddy and Ralph were up to. That had been, what? Three years before. It seemed longer. Now Charles was so tall and so serious that even Ralph had stopped treating him like a baby. Agnes flicked a piece of hay from her hem. Ralph.

A lowing off to the east made Agnes look up. In the long, narrow pasture that adjoined their garden plot on the far side, Mrs. Otto's cow was standing still, bawling at nothing. Dilly was swollen through the belly and flank—she was close to calving. Agnes liked Dilly—she was friendly and always put her head over the fence to be patted when Agnes worked in the kitchen garden.

Agnes glanced down at her diary. She had said so many awful things about Ralph in it lately. But how could he just leave them? How *could* he? He knew how much Daddy needed his help—how much they all depended on him.

Agnes stretched, enjoying her stolen minutes of

privacy and silence. Maybe Daddy would teach her to drive soon. She hoped so, but she doubted it. He hadn't taught Ralph until he was almost fifteen—he said they couldn't afford an accident. He had traded their Model T and two good cows for the panel truck a few years before and he was always working on it to keep it running.

Agnes heard Dilly bawling again and saw her stretching, switching her tail. Agnes wished Mr. Otto was still around. He had been a sweet, smiling man who told good stories. He had made his living in the coal mines as a young man, then had retired to truck farming in his later years when his lungs got bad. People knew his tomatoes by sight. They had a yellow patch on the blossom end that seemed to make them sweeter than anyone else's.

Mrs. Otto still saved seed every year—and she gave it only to people who would plant the tomatoes apart from any others to keep the strain pure. It was her husband's legacy, she always said. Agnes smiled. Mrs. Otto said a lot of things. She loved to talk. Agnes closed her diary and slipped it into her apron pocket and started to stand up. Then she heard Daddy shout and looked across the pasture toward the old wood-pile. He was hopping on one foot and she heard him curse. In his right hand, the hammer dangled loosely. Had he somehow hit himself in the foot while he was knocking the old lumber apart?

Agnes started toward him, but then he turned purposefully and walked in the direction of the house. He was limping badly, using his right leg to carry most of his weight, but he was walking *fast*. Agnes hesitated. When Daddy was hurt, especially if it was something that made him feel foolish, it was best to leave him alone for a while. And if he had hit his own foot with the hammer . . .

Agnes watched him go through the pasture gate into the barnyard. Then, instead of turning toward the porch, he walked straight uphill alongside the barn, passing the wide barn doors, heading for the milk house.

Agnes exhaled. He wasn't very hurt, or he'd have gone to the house. He'd probably just banged a toe with the hammer and was more angry than injured. She sat back down, then leaned against the hay, closing her eyes. Daddy was in a dark mood lately, that was sure, what with Ralph disappearing and money so tight. Mary had cried the night before because Daddy had scolded her for milking too slow. Of course, none of them could milk as fast as Ralph had.

Agnes heard the screen door slam, a distant, small sound, but unmistakable. She opened her eyes. Mary was standing in the dusty barnyard, her hands on her hips, her skinny arms akimbo. From here, she looked like a girl made out of toothpicks.

"Agnes? Agnesssssss!"

Mary's voice sounded brittle and thin, too, as the breeze carried it through the pinions at the low edge of the yard. Probably Mama wanted help with something before afternoon milking. Agnes sat very still, tucking her legs up against her chest, making herself small. All she wanted was a little more time to herself. She scrunched down, hoping Mary would turn and go back in—but she knew it wasn't likely. Mary wasn't giving up with just a quick look around. That meant Mama had some chore she wanted both of them to do—something Mary didn't want to do alone. Scrubbing more cucumbers for pickles, maybe, and packing the jars.

Agnes frowned. Or maybe it was something worse. Like weeding the lettuce patch or mucking the horses' stall. Whatever it was, Mary wasn't giving up. She was turning one way, then back, her hand up to shade her eyes.

Mary squared her shoulders suddenly and planted her feet, and Agnes knew that she had been spotted. Mary stood still a second longer, then began to run. She was halfway across the pasture, her long skinny legs pumping, when Agnes began to understand her words.

"Agnes, come quick. Mama says to come." Mary's voice was blurred by breathlessness and fear as she ran toward Agnes.

Agnes stood up. She started toward her sister,

her heart beating hard even before she started to run. As they met, Mary spun around, grabbing Agnes's hand and pulling at her until they were running hard for the house.

"What?" Agnes demanded as they slowed to pick their way through the chickens that were scratching at the soft soil on the shady side of their coop. The Leghorn rooster stiffened his wings and threatened them, but Mary brushed past him. "Daddy's hurt. He's lying down on the kitchen floor."

Before Agnes could react, Mary had jerked free and was running up the porch steps. The screen door banged open, then closed behind her. Agnes felt her stomach tighten as she followed, opening the door to go inside. She hesitated at the kitchen door, staring. Daddy was lying on the green linoleum. Charles was backed up against the refrigerator, his hands clenched around each other, his face white as the sheets on the line. Mary was beside him, her eyes wild and frightened.

"Agnes," Mama said tersely. "Come here and hold your father's hands."

CHAPTER TWO

Agnes nodded, not really understanding, and moved closer, her heart tight and painful in her chest. What was wrong? Mary was dancing back and forth now, one hand over her mouth, staring down at Daddy.

Daddy's head was tilted back, his eyes squeezed shut. Agnes swallowed, her stomach unsteady. "What happened . . . " she began.

Mama looked up sharply. "One of those long nails down by the barn. He drove it just about through his right heel."

Daddy cleared his throat. "I saw a snake and ran over like a fool to kill it with the hammer without looking where I was going." Agnes was relieved to hear his voice, even though it was roughened with pain. "Pull it out, Alice." He closed his eyes again.

"Here, Agnes," Mama was saying. "You sit here. Just hold onto his hands as tight as anything. Help him keep still."

Agnes obeyed, kneeling next to Daddy and taking

his hands from Mama. He held hers loosely and she could feel a tiny tremor in his muscles.

"You just keep quiet now, kids," he managed and his voice was terse, but almost normal. He rolled onto his side so Mama could reach the bottom of his foot easier. "It went right through the hole in the heel, Alice."

Mama nodded. "I see it." She spoke slowly, calmly, like she always did when someone was hurt. Mama had had a year of nurses' school before she quit to marry Daddy. She had been planning to finish her schooling up in Denver when the hard times hit.

"Wait, Grover," she said, letting him lower his foot. For the first time, Agnes noticed the fencing tool on the kitchen table—it usually hung from a hook in the milk house. Daddy must have tried to get the nail out by himself.

Abruptly, Mama got to her feet and went to open the bottom drawer of the Hoosier cabinet, where she kept the household tools. She lifted out a pair of small pliers and hefted them in her hand. Mary made a high squeal and ran to the door.

"Mary!" Mama's voice brought her to a stop. "Take your brother out into the yard with you and keep an eye on him." She paused. "I am depending on you."

Agnes glanced up from Daddy's tense face and saw Mary nod as she held out her hand and led

Charles along. Both of their faces were somber and worried as they went into the hall.

"Hold tight to Agnes, Grover," Mama was saying as she knelt beside Daddy's feet. "It's going to be hard for me to get a good grip on it. The way the boot sole is frayed, the head barely shows."

Agnes held her father's hand, staring at the dark hair on his wrist, the scars across his knuckles from his days as a country-fair prize-fighter. "Don't fiddle around, Alice," Daddy said in his almost-normal voice, and he opened his eyes again. "You just do what you have to do."

Then Mama bent over his boot and he fell silent. Agnes saw his eyes close, and his lips thinned as he set his jaw. A second later, a terrible sound came from his opened mouth, like his voice was being dragged from his throat against his will. His grip tightened, crushing Agnes's hands into knots. He thrashed sideways, then curled forward, half sitting. He slumped back when Mama straightened.

"I couldn't . . . I didn't get it," Mama said. Her voice was unsteady now. "Where the leather is torn, it's hard . . . Oh, I am so sorry, Grover."

Daddy wrenched into a sitting position and jerked the pliers out of her hand. Agnes sat back as he tucked his legs beneath himself, almost kneeling, then reached around. He struggled to turn his head far enough to see, clumsily trying to position the pliers over the nail. The wound was bleeding now, Agnes saw. Not much. Just a trickle. It stained the edges of the hole that hard work and time had worn in Daddy's boot heel.

Agnes watched, powerless to move, but desperate to leave the kitchen, to run outside, away from her father's pained face and quickened breathing. Where was Ralph? She wanted him here, now, at home. She didn't want to be the oldest one. If Ralph had still been here, Mama would have called him to hold Daddy still—and he might have managed it.

There was a tapping sound at the door and Agnes looked up, half expecting to see Ralph standing there. But of course it wasn't. It was the big white rooster, pecking up a grain or two of corn spilled from Mama's shucking the night before. Agnes wished with all her heart Ralph *would* just show up at the door. It was like an ache inside her, swelling to fill up every corner of her thoughts. If he did, she could go stand outside with Charles and Mary to wait instead of having to be here, watching Daddy contorted awkwardly, holding the pliers in one hand and his own ankle in the other.

He grunted in pain as he tried to get the nail head between the metal jaws, then winced. He lifted the pliers, readjusting his grip on them. Then he started again. Agnes saw beads of sweat rising on his forehead as his cheeks went pink with effort. A strand of his dark hair hung in the center of his forehead. The house seemed unnaturally quiet. Mama was as still as a stone. Grandfather's tall clock ticked into the silence. Agnes counted fifty ticks, then fifty more as Daddy worked with the pliers, fighting the awkwardness of his position.

"I can't do it," he finally exploded. His face dark with pain and anger, he flipped the pliers sideways. The handles opened and they spun across the linoleum like a lopsided star, sliding under the sink and striking the wall.

Agnes scuttled after them as her mother tried to calm Daddy, asking him to lie back down, murmuring a constant stream of soothing words. Agnes reached for the pliers, careful not to bump her head against the bottom of the sink. It was rose-colored porcelain, her mother's pride before the hard times had come on. Now, Agnes was sure they would never get the modern, electric range and the bigger refrigerator her mother had dreamed of adding to modernize the kitchen.

As she stood up, Agnes glanced out the screen door. Mary and Charles were standing on the porch, holding hands. Agnes could hear Mama saying something in an urgent, low voice behind her.

"We can't afford it!" Daddy exploded.

"You need a doctor," Mama answered, her voice shrill.

Agnes spun around to see him half sitting again.

His eyes were glittery, strange. "He'll call me an idiot for working in a barnyard with holes in my boots," Daddy said through gritted teeth. "Then he'll pocket the money and laugh all the way home about what a fool—"

"Stop it, Grover," Mama cut in. She began to lecture him again, one hand spread flat on his chest. Agnes glanced back out the door. Mary was alone now. Charles had gone off to play or to cry.

Suddenly, Daddy lay back down. Mama motioned at Agnes, reaching out and snapping her fingers. The sharp little sound brought Agnes back from her drifting thoughts. She took a step forward to give her mother the pliers.

"You hold him still this time," Mama said in a whisper.

Agnes nodded and knelt beside Daddy once more. He took her hands carefully, gently, like he was afraid he would hurt her, but more afraid he'd jump if he didn't have anything to hang on to.

"Hold tight," Mama said again.

This time, Daddy made no sound at all, except a long whooshing of breath. His mouth stretched into a silent cry, though, with parallel furrows along his mouth and fanning out from his eyes that made him look like someone else—someone Agnes had never seen before. It scared her.

"One more pull," Mama said quietly, and Daddy

grunted, letting her know that he had heard her. Agnes could see the nail protruding now, about a half inch. Mama had managed to work it free of the peeling boot heel. Agnes watched her mother lower the pliers one more time and felt Daddy tense against the pain.

He moaned a little, but kept his lips pressed together, his eyes closed hard. His grip on Agnes's hands was agonizingly tight for a few seconds. Then he relaxed, sagging back to the floor.

Agnes turned to see her mother staring at a long, bloody nail, pinched between the jaws of the pliers. "Now, we'll want to wash it out," Mama said. Her voice sounded weak, but steady.

Agnes stood up slowly, backing toward the door. Her diary swung against her belly and she remembered, for the first time, that she had it with her. Usually she hid it in the barn before she came to the house. No one knew about it except Mama, and she thought it was a keepsake book, not a diary.

"Aggie, move the herd to the alfalfa pasture," Daddy said, looking at her, taking slow, ragged breaths as he sat up. He was silent a moment, then got to his feet awkwardly and walked, herky-jerky, to drop into a kitchen chair. Mama was filling a washbasin at the sink pump.

"I ought to be able to go back to work in an hour or two," Daddy said, wincing as he lifted his foot to rest it across his other leg, like men sat when they whittled. But he lowered it again as though the change had only made it hurt more. He looked at Agnes. "Can you help a little extra?"

She nodded. "I'll take care of the cows, Daddy."

He motioned for her to go, an impatient, weary gesture.

Agnes retreated to the door, then turned around again. It was hard to walk away, to stop staring at his face. He looked pale and weak, but at least he looked familiar again. It had been so awful, that misshapen grimace that had made him seem like a stranger.

"We have to wash it out," Mama was saying again as Daddy pulled off his boot, bending his knee to look at the wound. He glanced up and noticed Agnes and straightened his leg, tipping his toes toward himself for her to see the sole of his foot.

Agnes saw his forced smile, and smiled back. It was a tiny wound, after all. Barely big enough to see. The thin trickle of blood was the only thing that marked the place where the nail had gone in.

Daddy shook his head. "Doesn't look like much, does it?"

"We ought to go see Doc Lammee," Mama began, but Daddy waved his hand dismissively. He was breathing normally now. He wiped his sleeve across his forehead. Only the pinched corners of his eyes belied how much pain he was still in.

"We can't afford it. Corsetino's lowered his

prices just enough to make the Alpine Rose and Shaski's Fireside think about switching their accounts to him. If we lose the restaurants . . . "

Agnes heard Mama clear her throat, and she glanced up. Mama's eyebrows were arched, her chin high. Daddy nodded. "All right, Alice. All right." He looked at Agnes. "Your mother thinks you worry too much about things that she and I are the ones to take care of."

Agnes heard her mother's impatient sigh. "Grover, she is just a child—"

"You were raised never to worry about anything, Alice," Daddy said, interrupting her. "But times are different now."

Agnes knew what was coming. Her parents had had this argument many times. It usually made Mama cry if it went on long enough. It seemed unfair. It wasn't Mama's fault she had been raised rich. Daddy made it sound like some kind of problem, like something bad.

Mama's father had been a dentist in Denver. So she had grown up with a maid and a cook and fine clothes and she had never had to worry about money when she was little. Daddy's folks had been ranchers. They lived north of town in an unpainted house near the railroad tracks now. Grampa had a very bad back, from all his years shearing sheep. He could barely walk some days.

Mama's voice rose and pulled Agnes out of her thoughts.

"I just don't want them—especially the girls—to spend their carefree years—"

"I never had any," Daddy interrupted her. "Alice, do you want them to make their way, or end up in a shelter somewhere on relief?"

"Grover Cleveland Gleason," Mama said, raising her voice a little higher. "Don't you say such a thing. No one in my family has ever—"

"Nor mine," Daddy interrupted. "And I will die working before I accept government help. But these children—"

"Go do as your father told you," Mama said, suddenly lifting one hand to stop Daddy midsentence.

He hesitated, startled into silence, then nodded. "Go on, Agnes." He rubbed absently at his ankle, and for a second, Agnes imagined the awful pain of the nail going into his foot. He cleared his throat. "I want the cows to get an hour or so of pasture, no more than that. The alfalfa is dangerous soft and green like this, and I don't want any bloating. Drive them back into the barn paddock for next milking. And keep an eye on the Jersey cow, she's close to calving."

"Inspector's coming next week, Agnes," Mama reminded her.

"I know," Agnes said, hoping her mother wouldn't start *that* up now, with Daddy already upset.

The inspector came once a month and lately Daddy was worried about failing the tests. Most of their cows were high-producing Holsteins that gave lower fat milk—and lots of it. So, as long as Agnes could remember, they had kept four Jerseys, mixing their high-fat milk into the bottling tanks to meet the legal butterfat standards. But now, they had only three Jerseys. Their best one had died in April—a piece of swallowed wire in her rumen—and they were barely passing the tests.

Agnes knew their Holsteins were nowhere near the legal 5 percent butterfat standard. That's what Mama was telling her. Keep an eye on the Jerseys because they couldn't stand the loss. Without the Jerseys, they'd fail the government tests and the dairy would be shut down—and they could not possibly afford to replace her.

"Go on," Daddy said again, shooing at her with one hand.

Agnes looked once more at the little tear in his skin and tried to smile. "I'm going, Daddy."

He reached down to pick up his sock and boot. "You're a lot of help to your mama and me, especially now that . . . " he trailed off, glancing at Mama. She was listening.

"Take Mary and Charles with you, please," Mama said.

Agnes turned, one hand inside her apron pocket

on her diary. She pushed open the screen. Mary came running toward her and Charles wasn't far behind. They clumped up the porch steps, their eyes fastened on her face. She tried to erase the worry from her eyes and her voice.

"Mama says you two are to help me with the cows."

CHAPTER THREE

"Is Daddy all right?" Mary asked breathlessly, leaning around Agnes to peer through the screen door. Charles stopped halfway up the steps, waiting for an answer.

"Yes," Agnes told them, forcing herself to smile. "Mama got the nail out of his foot, and you can barely even see a mark."

"I was scared," Mary said quietly.

Charles shook his head. "I wasn't." He hooked his thumbs through his suspenders and looked like a comical miniature of Ralph—or Daddy. Agnes almost laughed, then didn't because she knew he was only acting tough to keep from admitting how scared he had been.

"We have to turn the cows out on the alfalfa," Agnes told them. She could hear her parents murmuring to each other in the kitchen. She fought an urge to go back in, to reassure herself that Daddy was all right. But she knew it would only worry Mary and

Charles if she acted like she wasn't sure. She grabbed Mary's hand and turned her around.

"Mama says you have to help."

"Me, too?" Charles asked.

"Yes." Agnes pulled Mary gently along, down the steps, then across the yard to the gate. Charles looked worried, and kept glancing back toward the house, but as Agnes went through the yard gate and started across the barnyard, he followed. A few paces farther on, Mary pulled her hand free and ran ahead, then circled back, bounding like a puppy all the way to the first pasture gate.

"Catch up with Mary," Agnes told Charles. "I'll go the other way and be right there." As he went on, she ducked into the barn through the double doors that faced the house. For a second, her sunstruck eyes saw nothing but dark shadows, then they began to adjust. She crossed to the horses' stall and hid her diary in its usual place behind the grain barrel, glancing up to make sure Charles hadn't come back for some reason.

Agnes heard the cows milling around the far end of the barn—they were in the big paddock just outside the other set of doors. Slats of sunlight streamed in between the planking.

The horses nickered and Agnes stopped to pat Blaze's wide forehead. Franklin, the tall, handsome gray gelding Mama had named after the president, stood aloof by the far wall as always. Agnes liked him.

He wasn't mean, he just wasn't friendly. Behind him, the horses' paddock door was shut. Agnes climbed over the rail and crossed the deep straw bedding to open it. Blaze somehow nudged her way past Franklin and was outside first. Agnes patted the gelding's flank as he followed. He twitched his skin as always, surprised and irritated at her touch.

"You've both forgotten what it's like to work every day since the snow melted, haven't you?" Agnes asked them. Blaze looked back inside. "It's been almost four months since you had to pull a load of hay, hasn't it?"

"Daddy said he might sell them," Mary said from outside the stall. Startled, Agnes turned to face her.

"Really? He still uses them to pull the hay sled all winter. The truck can't do that."

Mary shrugged. "I hope not. We shouldn't have to sell *everything*."

"What are you doing in there?" Charles called from the far end of the barn. The doors opened suddenly and he slipped inside.

"Are you sure that Daddy is all right?" Mary asked as he walked toward them.

Charles made a sound of dismissal. "Why wouldn't he be all right? You're dumb."

Agnes leaned and tapped the top of his head. "No, she isn't. You be nice."

He stretched up tall and glared at her. "You can't tell me what to do."

Agnes shook her head. "Charles, just be nice. Come on." She climbed back over the railing and led the way down the wide center aisle.

The cement gutter that ran along beside the stanchions needed washing. Agnes wrinkled her nose at the strong, sharp odor of manure. It had been one of Ralph's chores that Daddy had been doing on top of his own work. He hadn't managed to get to it before he hurt himself. Now he wouldn't.

Agnes sighed. Maybe she should begin washing down the cement gutter after every milking. Mama certainly didn't have time. Without Ralph's help, it was all she could do to get the milk cooled down and bottled and the cream separated before Daddy began deliveries every morning.

Agnes pushed open the far doors. The cows looked up sharply, startled by the sudden appearance of three people in their midst. But their surprise lasted only a few seconds. Their deep brown eyes calm and trusting, they went back to picking at the hay in the long rick that ran along one whole side of the paddock.

"Get the gate, please, Mary," Agnes said.

Mary nodded and walked through the herd, touching her favorites as she passed. Butterscotch was first and got a solid pat on the shoulder. The old cow turned to watch Mary pass with huge, loving eyes. Mary always brought her bits of parsnips and carrot. Delilah, a big, ugly Holstein with a bony behind and hocks that rubbed together when she walked—and who was the best milker they owned—ducked her head, inviting an ear scratch. Mary gave her only a few seconds' worth and went on.

"Got it," Mary called, knowing that Agnes couldn't see with the herd between them.

"All right, ladies," Agnes said, clapping her hands, talking to the cows the way her father always did. "Let's go eat a little alfalfa before milking, shall we?"

"They don't understand you," Charles said.

"Yes, they do," Agnes said firmly. "Every word."

Charles giggled. "Tell them they have to milk themselves tonight, then." He laughed. "Tell them how to run the bottler and the steam table."

Mary laughed from her post by the gate. "I'll go open the pasture gate," she called.

"All right," Agnes answered. "Charles and I will get them moving."

She clapped her hands and started forward, Charles beside her, widening his arms to shoo the big gentle cows. It didn't take much effort. The cows had a good idea where they were going and it was fine with them. Slow-footed and patient, they began to pass through the paddock gate, stringing out in a line of twos and threes behind Mary, who ran ahead of them, her long hair jouncing over her shoulders with each stride.

Following the path, Agnes tried to whistle,

glancing every few seconds at Charles. His face was somber again, and she wondered what he was thinking. He had helped more with milking since Ralph had left than he had ever had to before in his life. Did he mind? Agnes glanced down into the gully as they passed it. The cottonwoods had all leafed out, and they twinkled as the breeze stirred them. Ralph had planted the corn patch at the far end the year before. This spring, Mama had had to do it. Even from here, Agnes could see weeds growing around the foot-high corn plants.

Without meaning to, Agnes suddenly pictured the awful, bloody nail held tightly in the pliers. She shivered as Mary came skipping back toward them, staying to one side of the plodding line of cows headed for the lower pasture.

"I stood the gate wide open." She was a little out of breath.

Agnes turned and nodded. "Good."

"Where do you think Ralphie is right now?" Mary asked.

"He's Ralph, not Ralphie," Charles said, echoing something they had all heard about a thousand times. Ralph had started hating his baby name at about fourteen.

"I bet he's working in one of the mines," Mary went on when no one else spoke. "Living up in the Walsen mine camp or one of the others."

Agnes shook her head. "He told me he didn't want to work underground."

Mary glanced up at her. "Lots of men do, though."

Agnes nodded. It was true. There were men from about every country in the world working in the mines, it seemed like. Daddy said some of the mines were closing though.

"I bet he's sitting in the Alpine Rose right now, eating meat loaf and pie," Mary said wistfully.

"How? He hasn't got any money," Agnes said sharply, and was immediately sorry because Mary ducked her head, embarrassed.

"I think he's in Pittsburgh." Charles sounded so matter of fact, like thinking about anyone they knew being in Pittsburgh was an everyday situation.

Mary lifted her head, smiling at him. "Pittsburgh." She giggled. "You don't even know where that is."

Charles bristled. "Kelly has an uncle there. He told me."

"But you don't know where it is, do you?" Mary teased. "Have you even seen it on the school map?"

Charles hesitated, then shook his head. "But he could be there."

Agnes found herself walking faster, lengthening her stride to get away from their bickering. It was stupid, all of it, everything they were talking about was silly. Nothing mattered except that Ralph was gone and Daddy was hurt.

By the time the last of the cows had passed through the gate, she was ready to close it. She counted the herd without thinking, starting over when Betsy kicked up her heels and lumbered a few strides, causing ten or twelve other cows to shift positions. Once she was sure that all thirty-nine cows were safely grazing on the alfalfa, she turned back to Mary and Charles.

"I'm going to go wash the manure gutters," she said. "So we don't have to do the evening milking in a mess."

Mary grimaced. "We don't have to help, do we? I'm tired. I had to wash all the dishes by myself and—"

"You did not," Charles interrupted. "I helped."

"You put them away, but you didn't—"

"Be quiet!" Agnes shouted at them, feeling their shrill voices like sandpaper against her skin. She started back toward the barn.

CHAPTER FOUR

Agnes opened the barn doors and walked into the cool, still building without looking back. Let them go play before supper, she thought angrily. They had worked so hard all day! Did they think that she hadn't? The only time she hadn't spent working at one chore or another had been the fifteen minutes or so when she had hidden out by the haystack.

Agnes started to uncoil the hose, then stopped and crossed to the horses' stall to pat Blaze and scratch her ears. Agnes traced the wide white streak that ran from the center of the mare's forehead down to her jaw. It was snow white against her red brown coat.

"I feel like I am going to blow up," Agnes whispered into the mare's ear. Blaze shook her head and Agnes smiled. "Yes, I really do. Don't you argue with me."

Blaze lifted her head, then lowered it, rubbing her jaw against Agnes's shoulder. Agnes braced herself against the sudden friendly pressure. Blaze rubbed harder, using Agnes as a scratching post, nearly pushing her over. Agnes finally laughed. "You don't much care what I feel like, do you?"

Blaze dropped her head, blowing out a soft breath through her nostrils—a calm, whiffling sound. "All right, you do," Agnes gave in, tugging at her forelock. Blaze leaned over the gate, reaching toward the broken bale of alfalfa. Agnes picked up a thick flake of the flowery-smelling hay and dropped it into the hayrick. That brought Franklin to life, and he walked over to make sure he got his share.

Agnes turned away from the stall, scolding herself. Things would work out, Mama always said. And they always had. Agnes unwrapped the hose from the old wheel Daddy had made into a hose spool. Then she turned the faucet on full blast and twisted the nozzle down tight so the stream of water narrowed and hit the trough hard.

As she worked, Agnes was careful to keep the stream of water at a low angle. She had learned the trick around Christmastime when Daddy and Ralph had both been sick with influenza for a few days and she'd had to wash the gutters. A sharp angle made the water spread into a ricocheting fan, spattering manure everywhere. Held low, the hard stream of water became a liquid broom, sweeping the gutter clean, washing the manure down the incline and out of the barn. The cement gutter ran in a curve toward the gully and dumped out at the bottom. Once the manure turned good and brown over the winter, it had been Ralph's job to shovel it onto the wagon bed and haul it up to the garden before Mama planted in the spring.

"Maybe I'll have to do that, too, now," Agnes groused as she pulled the hose along down the long row of stanchions, out the doors, and twenty feet or so past the barn. Where the gutter steepened, the water whisked the manure along without the steady hard stream shoving at it. Agnes kinked the hose and looked around. Mary and Charles had gone in—or were fooling around somewhere. She sighed, dragging the hose back through the hay and dust. She turned off the water, then coiled the hose, turning the faucet on to wash her hands once she was finished.

"Agnes?"

"Yes?" She whirled around at the sound of Mama's voice. Mama came toward her, keeping clear of the mud where the water had slopped over the edge of the cement gutter.

"I'm going to take your father into town to see Doctor Lammee."

"I thought he said he didn't need—"

"We'll be back in an hour or so," Mama interrupted her, and Agnes was startled by the sharpness in her voice. "I need you to take care of your brother and sister—" Mama broke off, looking around. "Where are they?"

Agnes shrugged. "They helped me take the cows down to pasture, then they ran off to play or something. I just noticed the gutter being dirty so I—"

"Find them and make sure that Charles puts on a sweater when it starts to cool off. You and I will have to milk late, I suppose."

"But, Mama," Agnes began, but her mother cut her off with a quick motion of her right hand and a fierce frown.

"I don't need anything more to worry about this evening, Agnes. Just take care of things until we can get home."

Agnes nodded, watching her mother turn and hurry back out the wide doors at the other end of the barn. "Mary? Charles!" Agnes called as she came out into the paddock, cupping her hands around her mouth. They weren't anywhere in sight. She walked far enough to see down into the gully, and shouted again. No answer.

Agnes heard the truck growling, the engine coming to life. A second later there was the steady puttering roar that meant it was safely started. She could hear her father's voice, from the house, shouting something to Mama, then the solid slam of the truck door told her he had gotten in. If he was letting Mama drive, Agnes knew it meant that his foot was hurting terribly. He didn't like Mama's driving. The sound of the engine faded as the truck left the drive and went down Elder Street toward town.

"Charles! Mary!" This time Agnes's shout was loud enough to echo off the hillside that rose to the west, but there was no other answer. She half turned, hoping that they would come skipping out from behind the haystack or leaping up out of one of the irrigation ditches. But they didn't. She squinted, scanning the pastures.

Maybe, Agnes thought suddenly, they were in the house. It was unlikely, she knew, since Mama hadn't seen them. But it was possible, especially if they were hiding upstairs, trying to stay out of the way. Hoping, she started toward the porch.

The screen door was ajar and Agnes pulled it open, pushing the door inward. "Mary? Charles?" The only sound was the ticking of the tall clock in the hall-way. Agnes went into the kitchen and washed her hands in Mama's rose-pink sink. She dried them on the old embroidered tea towel hanging from its hook just over the dish drain, then turned around again. Maybe they were playing a trick on her.

Agnes went down the hall into the front room, then turned to go upstairs. If they were hiding, she was going to be furious with them. If they jumped out and startled her now, she was going to throw a tizzy.

At the top of the stairs, Agnes stopped and

listened again. The house was quiet, except for the usual creaks and pops in the wooden walls. She called Mary's name and waited. Nothing. Walking fast, she went down the upstairs hall, looking into the boys' room, then her own and Mary's, then checking the little storeroom under the eaves. The slanted ceiling made it hard to stand up, but she looked over the boxes of winter linens and sweaters packed in mothballs just the same. They weren't here.

Agnes went back down the stairs in a quick, noisy staccato rhythm. She clumped through the living room and out into the downstairs hall that led past the kitchen. She banged out the back door and stood in the yard again. The chickens were over along the fence. She would have to remember to close the coop door this evening if Mama and Daddy weren't home before sunset. There had been coyotes sniffing around the yard lately while everyone was asleep. They wouldn't bother the cows or the pigs, but they would kill chickens if they got a chance.

Agnes put her hands on her hips, wishing Charles and Mary would just appear. They hadn't had enough time to go very far, and they knew Daddy was hurt and—Agnes turned to face the haystack. Maybe they were hiding like she did sometimes. She set off across the yard, walking fast, calling their names as she opened the gate into the barnyard. At the bottom of the incline, past the barn, she opened the pasture gate, then called again. Halfway across the field, she stopped.

"Mary?" she yelled, facing the pastures, then she turned and yelled again, facing the yard. "Mary?"

"We're over here!"

Agnes exhaled at the sound of Charles's voice, even though she couldn't spot him. He yelled again. They were down in the gully, she realized as she took a slanting path back up out of the pasture and turned to skirt the paddock below the barn, following the cement gutter.

"I didn't mean to," Charles shouted before she was close enough to see the expression on his face— but his voice sounded tight and strained.

Agnes sprinted, racing along the rim of the gully past the big cottonwood tree that held their rope swing. As she got closer, Charles turned and ran down the slope. She followed him, taking short, choppy strides down the steepest part. His face was flushed as he slowed where the ground flattened out.

"Where's Mary?"

He pointed and Agnes saw her sister step out from behind a tree. "I'm here, Aggie."

Agnes stared into Mary's face, scanning her clear white skin for blood, for a bruise, for some sign of hurt. Her eyes were red. She had been crying hard.

"Mama is going to be so upset," Charles was saying.

Mary nodded unhappily as she turned around,

looking at Agnes over her shoulder as she did, her cheeks pinkened with her crying. Suddenly, Agnes understood. The back of Mary's dress was torn—a terrible tear almost a foot long, right above the hemline.

"Mama can probably fix it or patch it," Agnes began, then she fell silent at the agony on her sister's face.

"This is supposed to last me till school, Aggie. You know how I'll get laughed at and Mama—"

"It was my fault," Charles said in a low voice.

"We were playing tag, running downhill. He stepped on it from behind and—"

"It just tore," Charles finished. "We heard you but Mary didn't want me to answer yet."

"I didn't want Mama to see it. She's already so upset with Daddy hurt and—"

"Mama took Daddy to the Lammees' hospital in town," Agnes interrupted, and saw the worry bloom in Mary's eyes. Charles squared his shoulders and stood a little taller—a clear sign that he was feeling scared.

"They'll be back before milking, or they'll try to," Agnes told them, staring at the long rip. "I could sew it up. Mama would see the mend, but if it was already fixed, she wouldn't have to find the time to do it, at least."

"*Could* you?" Mary asked. "Oh, Agnes, I would be so grateful. Maybe she wouldn't notice until laundry day and by then Daddy will be all right and everything will be better."

Agnes nodded. "Let's go up to the house."

They climbed up out of the gully, then walked alongside it, wrinkling their noses as they came close to the end where the manure gutter dumped out.

As they went in the back door, Agnes let out a breath of pure relief. Nothing bad had happened besides the torn dress. Mama would be very upset—they didn't have a spare penny for clothes—but at least Mary hadn't been hurt.

"I'll run and get Mama's sewing basket," Mary said. "If you can get it mended before they get back—"

"I'll try," Agnes told her. "But you two have to help me bring the cows up in a while."

"We will," Mary promised, and Charles echoed her words as he turned into the kitchen. Agnes could hear him rummaging around, looking for some little leftover in the refrigerator that Mama might have forgotten. Agnes knew he wouldn't find anything besides the big pot of beans they had been eating for a week. Mama said beans were good food and cheaper than anything. She peeked in the door and watched him. He finally took one of the little red cabbages out of Mama's garden basket and leaned over the sink to bite into it. He ate it like an apple. In seconds, it was gone.

"Friday is inspector day," Agnes said.

"That's good," Charles said, smiling broadly.

Agnes understood him instantly. There would be meat of some kind on Friday. When the inspector came, he stayed overnight and left early the next morning after testing the milk. So they usually had company food for supper, maybe sausage or a ham. That was the only good thing about the inspector coming.

"There's a blue thread that ought to match," Mary was saying, coming down the stairs. Agnes turned to look down the hall at her.

They sat down in the front room and Mary threaded the needle, then turned around so that Agnes could turn the back of her dress up far enough to sew from the wrong side of the cloth. With Mary fussing and wiggling, it took longer than it needed to and the stitches weren't as straight or as small as Agnes would have liked, but it would hold. She smoothed Mary's skirt and watched her whirl around the room.

"Thank you, Agnes. Mama won't get as upset now, I just know it."

Just then, the phone rang. Mary stopped mid-step. They all listened to see whose ring it was. The first ring ended and there was a little pause. Another ring came from the bell box on the wall, short and defined, like a burst of water. A second later, there was a third ring, then a fourth. Then there was silence. Four rings—that was their line. Agnes raced to pick up the receiver.

CHAPTER FIVE

"Alice?"

Agnes recognized the voice instantly. "Hello, Mrs. Otto. This is Agnes. Mama isn't here right now."

"What?" Mrs. Otto asked sharply.

Agnes covered the mouthpiece with her hand. "It's just Mrs. Otto," she whispered to Charles and Mary. Then she swung the heavy receiver back up to her mouth. "Mother isn't here just now," she said, louder and more clearly. Mrs. Otto was a little deaf.

"Well, then, please send your father over, Agnes. Is he out in the field where you can find him?"

Agnes turned, wrapping the phone cord around her arm. "He isn't here either, Mrs. Otto."

"Ralphie then? I need help badly, Agnes, or I wouldn't ask."

"Is anything the matter?" Agnes asked, partly to avoid telling Mrs. Otto that Ralph wasn't there either.

"Dilly is having trouble."

Agnes crossed her fingers. "What sort of trouble, Mrs. Otto?"

"Calving. She's been down in her stall for almost two hours, straining hard. I think she's getting weak."

Agnes shivered. She had watched her father and brother help cows give birth many times. But she had always been the one to run and fetch buckets of water or bundles of rags—Ralph and Daddy were the ones to make decisions.

"Agnes?" Mrs. Otto's voice was shrill.

"Yes, ma'am."

"Are you there? I need help with Dilly."

"I'll . . . be right there," Agnes said.

"Hurry then, dear. And tell Ralph I am sorry to bother him."

"But—" Agnes began. There was a sharp click as Mrs. Otto hung up. Agnes replaced the receiver, settling it into the deep cradle and pushing them back toward the bell box on the wall. Charles and Mary were staring at her.

"What did she want?"

"Dilly is having trouble calving." Agnes saw Mary frown and remembered how much she liked the old dark yellow Guernsey. "I think everything will be all right, Mary. I just have to go see if I can help." She started toward the back door.

Charles shook his head. "But what about the cows?"

Agnes stopped mid-step. Of course. They were still on the alfalfa. How long had it been? Maybe if she just sat down in the living room and waited a while, Daddy would come limping through the door, a little hurt, but fine and perfectly able to go take care of Dilly and Mrs. Otto.

"What are we going to do?" Mary asked. Charles was fidgeting from one foot to the other.

"The two of you can bring in our cows," Agnes said, hesitating. "Just bring them up into the paddock and be sure to bar the gate."

"Okay," Mary said slowly. "But what if Mama and Daddy call while we are all outside?"

Agnes thought about it. "They won't, probably. If they do they'll just figure we're doing chores, or starting milking." She glanced up at the clock. It was barely two o'clock now, but if it weren't for Mrs. Otto needing help with Dilly, it would have been smart to start milking early. Mary was not a fast milker and Charles always got whiny toward the end. Without Daddy and Mama and Ralph . . . Agnes felt uneasy, knowing that so many things depended on her. "That's enough talk, now," she said firmly. "We have work to do."

Mary started down the hall, Charles close behind her. They banged open the screen door and Agnes watched them go out. It took her a few minutes to wash up and change into an old dress she used for her worst chores. It was tight across her shoulders and through the bodice, but Mama wouldn't care if anything happened to it. The cloth was worn and stained to the point of uselessness. Whenever it was finally cut up for the rag bag, there would be only a few squares to save for patches.

Agnes saw Mary and Charles in the alfalfa pasture as she veered across the home pasture, following the line of pinions. It was shorter to cut through the pastures than to go out the drive and along Elder Street.

Agnes liked Mrs. Otto. She had lived next door Agnes's whole life. She was so old now that Mama worried about her living alone. But her children had grown and moved off the farm, and her husband had died three years before. She wouldn't keep a hired hand—said she couldn't afford to.

Agnes glanced back before she ducked through the rail fence. Mary and Charles had the gate open and they were beginning to shoo the cows toward it. Usually, the cows would move toward the gate easily. But none of them wanted to stop grazing now. The lush green alfalfa was a rare treat.

Agnes straightened up, then hesitated on the far side of the fence, watching. Delilah, the biggest of the Holsteins, was sidling forward now. Two or three of the others moved along with her. Mary was shouting at them, flapping her skirt hem to get them started.

Charles was clapping his hands. They would manage. Agnes turned and started across the long narrow pasture that bordered Mrs. Otto's house.

The incline got steeper, but Agnes kept up her quick stride. She liked the Otto place with its huge old willow trees and the stone wall that ran along the front. Mrs. Otto's irises grew along it. They were in bloom now, the grape scent heavy in the air around them.

"Come on," Mrs. Otto called to her, coming out the front door, tying a scarf beneath her chin. Mrs. Otto's hair was thin and she didn't like people to notice. She still had the prettiest eyes in Huerfano County, Daddy said, and it was true. Her eyes were the color of May bluebells.

"I've been watching out the window for you. Where's Ralph?" She had an old towel folded beneath one arm. When Agnes looked aside and didn't answer, Mrs. Otto started toward the barn.

Agnes followed silently, reluctant to tell the truth. Mama and Daddy might not want the whole town to know that Ralph had left. And if she told Mrs. Otto, the whole town *would* know by morning. Mrs. Otto had been the telephone operator for years, and she was a friendly, good-hearted gossip who was interested in everyone's affairs. Proud new grandparents often found that there was no one left to tell—their neighbors had already heard the news from Mrs.

Otto. People with secrets sometimes heard their private business whispered at church. But everyone forgave Mrs. Otto for meddling because the result was usually worth the embarrassment. Arguments were mended, things got out into the light to be solved.

"Where's Ralph?" Mrs. Otto asked again, in a louder voice as she stood aside to let Agnes go into the barn first.

"He . . . um . . . he can't come," Agnes said, walking quickly down the long center aisle to Dilly's stall. There were no cement gutters here, no stanchions. The Ottos had never run dairy cows.

Mrs. Otto was looking at Agnes sharply. "Can't come?"

Agnes shook her head. "No, ma'am."

Dilly was down in the straw, her coat stained with sweat. She was lying stretched out and as Agnes watched, a convulsion took the cow and she strained, stretching out her neck.

"She's been at it far too long," Mrs. Otto said.

"I'm not sure what to do," Agnes admitted. "Daddy always says you should just let nature do it if you can."

"Nature is going to kill my good old cow," Mrs. Otto said sharply. "If I let her." She sighed. "If I could bend over with any hope of standing up on my own again, I would never have called you. See if the calf is straight inside her."

Agnes bit her lip. "I've seen Daddy do it, but—"

"Not a thing in the world hard about it," Mrs. Otto said.

Agnes went around to Dilly's tail and knelt in the straw. She leaned forward and felt along her flank, running her hand over the cow's coat, closing her eyes like she had seen Daddy do. Inside Dilly, she could feel a jerking motion. But the motion was muted by the bulk of Dilly's body, like someone moving beneath a stack of blankets.

Agnes glanced up.

Mrs. Otto was staring at her. "Can you feel the position the baby is in?"

Agnes shook her head.

"The legs are sharper, like bent twigs or something. The head feels bigger and rounder and it should be toward Dilly's hind end now."

Agnes shook her head again. Where was Daddy? Or Ralph or *anyone* but her? She tried running her hands across Dilly's flank again. It was all lumps and bumps and nothing felt like *anything*. "I can't tell," she said.

"Help me, then," Mrs. Otto said. She held out her hand. Agnes stood and supported her as she sank awkwardly to her knees beside Dilly. She ran her hands over the old cow's flank and Dilly looked up, arching her neck, breathing hard.

"We are here to help you, Dilly-girl," Mrs. Otto assured her. "Here to make your job easier if we can."

Agnes watched the old woman rub at Dilly's belly with the flat of her hand. "I don't think anything is amiss." She took Agnes's hand and placed it on Dilly's flank. "Feel that?"

Suddenly there was a big, blunt bump beneath Agnes's hand. It pushed upward, then sank again. She had felt calves moving inside their mother's bellies before, but only for fun. She closed her eyes. "That's the head?"

"It is," Mrs. Otto said. "So it's pointed the right way. It's probably just big."

Agnes caught her breath. Sometimes, when the calf was too big, the cow died because she couldn't push hard enough to make the baby come out. Daddy sometimes pulled a too big calf out, reaching up inside the cow to do it.

Agnes glanced sidelong at Mrs. Otto's thin arms. Her skin was like caterpillar skin, thin and wrinkly and fragile looking.

"Of course we can," Mrs. Otto said firmly to Dilly. "We can help." She turned her astonishingly blue eyes on Agnes and shook her finger. "You are not going to fail me and this old cow, young lady. I'd rather have Ralph or your father, but you're all I've got."

Agnes swallowed. "I'll try, but—"

"Try, nothing," Mrs. Otto cut her off. "That's the one thing I leaned from Kurt dying," she said sharply. "When you have to, you don't try, you just *manage*."

Dilly made a grunting sound and her body stiffened again. Agnes could see the bulge moving inside her, sliding forward, then back. She told Mrs. Otto, and the old woman patted her shoulder.

"Exactly. Forward and back. She isn't making any progress, and she is almost exhausted."

Agnes watched Dilly lift her head once more, her deep brown eyes circled in white as she craned backward, looking at them. Agnes scooted closer to Mrs. Otto and watched as the cow strained. Just inside the birth opening, there was a tiny hoof that appeared, then receded again. Dilly lay flat, her sides heaving.

"It's a matter of strength, Agnes. You just get a firm hold on the baby and pull while Dilly pushes. I am not strong enough anymore. Help me up and I'll get out of your way now."

Agnes stood, offering Mrs. Otto her hand. The old woman got stiffly to her feet and swayed back and forth for a few seconds. "My old knees," she said, stepping to one side. She went to stand near Dilly's head, talking quietly to her.

Agnes knelt again. She set her jaw and when Dilly stiffened, she slid her hand inside the cow's birth passage. Instantly she felt the hard little heart shape of the calf's front hooves. She hooked her fingers around them and pulled gently. Nothing happened. After the contraction, Dilly lay flat, her breath whistling in and out of her nostrils.

When the cow arched her neck again, Agnes was ready. Pulling steadily on the calf's forelegs, she rocked back on her heels. This time, the little hooves slid into sight. Agnes grinned at Mrs. Otto.

"Good girl. Do it again." Mrs. Otto's blue eyes sparkled.

The next contraction brought Dilly's head up as she panted and strained. Agnes pulled again. This time the calf's tiny muzzle emerged and Mrs. Otto whooped—a very undignified, unladylike whoop. Agnes grinned up at her again.

"Keep your mind on your work," Mrs. Otto scolded her in a teasing voice, and Agnes looked back down, shifting her grip to the calf's neck.

Dilly pushed once more, panting hard, her long tongue lolling out as she strained. The calf was slippery with birth fluid and Agnes nearly lost her grip, but she managed to hang on. Dilly grunted with effort and the calf slid forward again, then, a second later, came completely into the world, landing in a heap in Agnes's lap.

Mrs. Otto handed Agnes the old towel and she used it to clean the baby's nostrils and mouth, then to dry her coat. The tiny heifer opened her eyes and wriggled, looking up at Agnes.

"She knows you saved her life," Mrs. Otto said. "Dilly does, too. Look."

Dilly was stretching her neck, reaching out

toward her calf, her ears forward. Agnes managed to stand, carrying the calf awkwardly against her stomach. Dilly made a whiffling sound, pulling in a deep breath full of the salty scent of her new daughter. She looked up straight at Agnes and blinked her huge brown eyes. Agnes set the calf in the straw beside her mother. Dilly turned and began to lick her baby dry. Agnes stood staring at them, startled when Mrs. Otto touched her shoulder.

"Whatever is wrong at home, you can handle it?"

Agnes looked at her. "I think so."

Mrs. Otto nodded. "Well, if not, you just give me a call. If I can't get there I'll raise Cain on the phone until someone else comes to help. A lot of people in this town owe me favors."

The calf was trying to stand up now, her legs disorganized. Agnes nodded without looking away from the pretty, perfect little heifer.

CHAPTER SIX

Agnes started home in a daze. How long had she been at Mrs. Otto's? As she climbed through the rail fence, she looked toward the house, hoping to see the panel truck parked out in front of the garden, but Mama and Daddy weren't home yet. Coming up through the pasture, she walked a little faster, listening for the sound of Mary's and Charles's voices.

Even if they hurried, with all three of them milking, it would still take a miracle for them to have the milk cooled and bottled before evening delivery time. Daddy would have to call Mr. Thomas, then load and leave the minute he got home. Even so, he would probably run out of daylight. That had happened a few times before, but Daddy didn't like it and neither did their customers. People wanted their milk fresh for suppertime.

Agnes glanced across the barnyard. The cows were in the paddock, shifting and bawling softly. They were more than ready to be milked, their udders heavy and uncomfortable. The big double doors on this end of the barn were closed, as were the upper doors. Agnes ran the last stretch, coming through the yard gate so fast that the rooster squawked and rushed his hens out of her way.

"Mary!" Agnes banged the screen door open. "Charles?"

"What happened at Mrs. Otto's?" Mary asked, pattering down the stairs and coming down the hall.

"Dilly has a little heifer," Agnes said. "We have to start milking now. Where's Charles?"

Mary shrugged. "I think in his bedroom."

Agnes frowned, a fluttery feeling rising in her stomach. She didn't want to be in charge. She didn't want to have to answer to Daddy for everything. "Mary, I need help," she said as calmly as she could. "You two could have had the cows in and washed up by now."

Mary ducked her chin and stared at her feet. "I thought maybe Mama or Daddy would telephone."

"They'll probably be home anytime now," Agnes said, hoping it was true. "But Daddy will wonder why we didn't start early since we knew milking would take longer with just the three of us. You know how slow Charles is."

Mary nodded. "Who'll carry the milk cans?"

Agnes hesitated. That was usually Daddy's chore. Or Ralph's, before he had left. "Me, I suppose. Go get Charles. I'll be out in the barn."

Mary ran back up the hall, and Agnes looked down at her soiled dress. There was little point in changing before she milked. And it wasn't like she had been handling a sick cow or anything. She rubbed her hands down her dress front, thinking about the first day of school and how embarrassed she was going to be if she only had her yellow dress and this one.

Maybe Mama could at least make her a flour-sack dress, something bright and new, even if it was homemade and old-fashioned. They had enough flour sacks, she was sure; it was just a matter of Mama finding the time amid all her other work. Agnes sighed, standing still and listening until she heard Charles answer Mary's calls. Good. He was upstairs.

Agnes went down the hall, pausing in the kitchen long enough to wash her hands, then opening the bread box. Chewing on a leathery heel—her favorite part of the loaf—she went out the back door. It would all be fine, she kept telling herself. Probably any second she would hear the clattering of the truck engine and the crunch of the gravel beneath the tires.

The back door banged open and Mary and Charles came running toward her. Together they walked across the barnyard. The cows were milling around in the barn paddock, still bawling. As Agnes opened the upper doors, Franklin and Blaze stepped up to the side of the stall, stamping their feet, whickering quietly. They were ready for their evening grain and some fresh hay.

"Open the end doors, Mary," Agnes called over the racket of the cows and the snorting of the horses. "Charles, will you get three buckets?" Without waiting, Agnes went to the wall pegs that held their milking stools. She took down Daddy's one-legged stool for herself, then a couple of three-legged ones for Mary and Charles to use. There were six stools. With Mama and Daddy and Ralph, they had sometimes needed them all.

As Mary ran around outside to shove the bar back and open the doors, Agnes set a stool beside each of the first three stanchions. Charles placed a big stainless-steel bucket beside each stool.

The cows came in, orderly and purposefully. They knew which twelve of them came first and there was no jostling or arguing: the order never changed. Teresa, a nearly all-black Holstein, led the way. She walked to the top stanchion and turned into it, putting her head between the slats. Agnes ran for grain.

The big tin bucket was on the wall with the Purina grain sack beneath it, a two-pound coffee can down inside. Agnes used the can to scoop grain into the bucket, counting a can and a half for each of the first twelve cows. They were coming through the doors at a good clip, their hooves clicking on the cement gutter as they stepped across it and settled themselves into their stanchions, nosing in their feed-boxes for grain.

As the last cow got herself positioned, Agnes began the rounds with the bucket, walking close to the wall, carrying the coffee can with her to scoop each cow's ration. Once the cows were eating contentedly, Agnes moved back up the line.

The stanchion boards came in pairs. The ones on the left could be moved back and forth, swinging on heavy steel pins drilled through the bottom end. The other was nailed into place, its top end holding a strap.

Agnes brought the first stanchion board up so that it was vertical, touching Teresa's wide neck on one side, the immovable board on the other. Unbuckling the strap with practiced hands, Agnes refastened it to hold the stanchion board in place. Now, even if she ran out of grain before they were finished milking her, Teresa would have to stand still. Her big, square-jawed head was trapped.

A clanging sound made Agnes look up to see Charles struggling with the first ten-gallon milk can. He settled the screen strainer across the top so that no flecks of hay or cow hair could fall into the clean milk.

"I have the BK solution made up," Mary called from the upper doors across from Blaze and Franklin's stall. She was carrying a steaming bucket so heavy it made her walk lopsided. She set it down and ran to the rag hamper by the wall, pulling out two hemmed squares of soft cotton.

Agnes smiled at her. The cows were stamping their feet as they ate, irritated by the weight of the milk in their udders. "Let's start," Agnes said. "Go as fast as you can, but don't run and don't spill milk. Charles, did you start the cooler?"

He shook his head and bolted out of the barn as Mary wrung out the rags in the bucket and the clean, sharp smell of the disinfectant rose with the steam. Working together, the girls had all the cows' udders washed by the time Charles came back in. "I put caps in the bottler, too," he announced, obviously proud of himself for thinking ahead.

Agnes smiled at him, imagining what she would tell Mama and Daddy about the way Charles and Mary had pitched in to get the work finished. They would be pleased to hear it. She glanced at the door on the way to pick up her stool and bucket. It'd be nice if her parents came home now and saw how all of them were doing their share. And then, of course, they would help. Daddy was the fastest milker, then Ralph, then Mama.

Agnes pushed thoughts of her brother and her parents aside. She sat down in one smooth motion, tucking the stool beneath herself as she bent her knees. It took practice to use the one-legged stool, but it was Agnes's favorite. It was easier to lean forward, then rock back, and her shoulders didn't get as tired. On the other hand, one little bobble in her balance and she might tip. She had even seen her father fall backward once, dumping a full bucket of milk in his startled attempt to grab something solid as he went over.

Teresa switched her tail the whole time, which was a nuisance, but she stood still. Agnes began milking, squirting the milk in little gushes into the steel pail. Teresa was an easy milker. The streams of milk came thick and fast, a ringing rhythm on the bottom of the empty bucket.

When she stood up to go empty her bucket, Agnes saw Mary milking at the next stanchion. Charles was at the third, milking Camel, the Jersey that had been named for her long, curving upper lip.

Agnes walked slowly to avoid splashing any milk onto the dirt floor. She lifted the bucket carefully, too. Then, with a smooth, quick motion, she poured it through the strainer into the widemouthed can, just fast enough so that not a drop was spilled.

"Daddy usually pours mine," Charles said from behind her. "I can't lift it high enough yet." Agnes turned to take his bucket. Charles didn't usually milk. He tended to the pigs and the chickens while they milked. Sometimes he helped with bottling.

"Thank you, Aggie," Charles said as she emptied his bucket. He scuttled back toward the cows and she watched him slide his stool forward, pushing the bucket beneath the cow.

Mary stood up and started toward the milk can, carrying her bucket carefully. She had gotten it too full and Agnes saw a little milk splash to the floor. Mary frowned.

"I'll take the first one in to cool," Agnes said. She switched the screen strainer to the next can, then bent to lift the full one. She couldn't.

"Maybe if we each take a handle we can do it," Mary said.

They stood on opposite sides and lifted on the count of three. It was still hard, but they managed to get the can into the milk house. It took two tries, but they got it up high enough to dump into the cooling tank.

Agnes stood for a second, shaking her head. "We better not fill them up."

Mary nodded. "Half full would be best, I think."

They started out the door. Agnes stopped suddenly and Mary bumped into her. "We should carry empties," Agnes explained.

"Let your head save your heels," Mary added. They both laughed. It was something Mama always said.

Agnes led the way, carrying two empty cans.

Mary brought back the one they had dumped, walking slowly. Charles was waiting with a full bucket of milk. Agnes dumped it for him, then hurried back to Teresa. She was half finished with her grain.

Agnes milked as fast as she could. Teresa was easy, but some of the others were much harder. The milk cans seemed to get heavier and heavier as they worked. They agreed to fill them halfway and still carried them in pairs. Charles helped, taking his turn at can carrying, but he had to go slower than Mary because he was smaller. Agnes had to bend over and walk crabwise to match his pace, but she managed.

Finally, Agnes loosed the stanchions and the first dozen cows filed without guidance to the upper doors. Agnes let them out. She broke open three bales of hay and filled the rack along the front fence. The cows settled in to eat.

Inside the barn, Mary had opened the lower doors again. Twelve more cows were sidling in, jostling for their regular places along the row of stanchions. Mary made up a fresh, steamy BK solution, and they started over.

By the time they were finished milking the fourth group—the smallest one, only three cows now that the Jersey had died—Agnes's hands and arms were aching. Mary and Charles set their stools back on the wall hooks and carried the last half can to the milk house.

"Mary," Agnes called as she finished hosing the bottom end of the manure gutter. "Charles?" She frowned as she kinked the hose and began to drag it back up to the faucet. "Mary!"

Still no answer.

Agnes washed the dust and splattered bits of manure from her hands. She hayed Blaze and Franklin, then went out the upper doors. The barn-yard was empty except for the chickens. Agnes walked up to the milk house to check the cooler. The water was running into the outside tank at a good rate and draining out the bottom hose just as fast. It wouldn't be long before the milk in the inner tank was chilled enough to bottle and cap.

Agnes sighed and glanced out the milk house doors toward the house. The back door was open and someone was standing at the sink. There was a sun glare on half the window and it was impossible to tell who it was.

Agnes smiled wearily. Maybe it was Mama! Her heart rose. If Mama and Daddy had gotten home, then she wouldn't have to finish up by herself and Daddy would have plenty of time to deliver before dark. She started toward the house, walking fast. Halfway across the yard, she heard the telephone ringing. Counting the rings, she broke into a run.

CHAPTER SEVEN

Agnes took the porch steps two and two, then sprinted across the planks, pulling the door wide as the phone rang for the fourth time. She knew instantly that Mama and Daddy were not in the kitchen, that they weren't home. Mary stood with one hand poised over the receiver, an anxious look on her face. When no fifth ring came, she snatched it up and held it out to Agnes.

"Hello," Agnes said, breathing hard from running, her heart thudding inside her chest.

"Hello? Agnes? It that you?"

The voice was unmistakable, and Agnes felt her shoulders sink, her heart begin to slow. "Yes, Mrs. Otto."

"Your parents called me about three quarters of an hour ago and said they couldn't raise you—"

"We were out in the barn milking," Agnes said, her heart quickening again.

"That's what your mother thought," Mrs. Otto

said, speaking with maddening slowness. "So she called me and asked me to call you kids until I got you. This is my fourth try."

Agnes waited, her hand tight around the receiver. "Are you still there?"

Mrs. Otto's voice was piercing and Agnes flinched. "Yes, ma'am. I just—what did Mama say?"

"Well, they won't be coming home, dear. Your mama and daddy are going on up to Pueblo tonight."

Agnes stood very still. "Pueblo?"

"Yes. Your father's tetanus immunization ought to protect him from the lockjaw, but Doctor Lammee was afraid he may have damaged his heel bones. Said he wanted the foot X-rayed on the Pueblo hospital machine—it's a better one than what they have here in Walsenburg, I guess. His brother thought it was best, too." Mrs. Otto paused and Agnes could hear her breathing for a second. "If both Lammees thought so, then it's likely good advice," she added, when Agnes didn't say anything.

Agnes didn't know what to say. No one in the family had ever had an X-ray. And Daddy wouldn't have cared if Doctor Lammee, his brother, and Franklin Delano Roosevelt thought he should have one—unless he thought so, too. His foot must really hurt for him to put up with the trouble and cost.

"That lockjaw, it's nothing to fool with," Mrs. Otto was saying. "I had an uncle who died of it back in ought-six. Uncle Jack. Lived his whole life up in Basalt. He was a miner. He just got sick and died in about ten days. It was quick—and he was a big, strong man."

"That's terrible," Agnes said. She could hear how faint and sad her voice sounded, but it had nothing to do with Mrs. Otto's Uncle Jack. "Daddy won't get tetanus, you said?"

"No, no, he's had the vaccine," Mrs. Otto murmured. "They didn't have it back then." She went right on talking about her uncle. Agnes half listened, thinking.

Mama and Daddy weren't coming home tonight. And anything to do with a hospital cost a lot of money. Mama would be upset and worried and scared. As Mrs. Otto went on with her story, Agnes turned toward the wall so that Mary and Charles couldn't see the fear in her own eyes. What if Daddy got laid up and couldn't work?

Agnes wished she could make the day start over. She would help Daddy with the woodpile, not hide. She would see the nail and warn him . . . She just wanted Mama and Daddy to come home *now*. She picked at the skirt of her dress, fighting tears.

"Your mother said to just pour out the night's milk and wash out the bottles."

Mrs. Otto's words startled Agnes out of her anxious thoughts. "We haven't even bottled yet. We just got finished milking and we—"

"Well, then, so much the better," Mrs. Otto said. "Your mother said they'd be home tomorrow, by evening milking, probably, and that you could just feed the pigs as much as they would take and then throw away the rest. But separate the cream, she said, and store what you can in the cool room."

Mrs. Otto paused. "If you want to send Ralph over with a few extra gallons tonight or tomorrow, my pigs could use extra."

"I'll try to do that, Mrs. Otto."

"What?" Mrs. Otto asked. Agnes raised her voice and repeated herself.

"Thank you," Mrs. Otto responded. "Your mother says she's called Mr. Thomas. She wants you to call the list of customers and explain why they aren't getting milk. She said to be extra polite."

"Mr. Grosvek will yell at me, sure," Agnes said. "He's grumpy when Daddy is ten minutes late."

Mrs. Otto made another sympathetic sound. "You just stay polite, no matter what he says."

Agnes frowned. They only dumped milk if one of the cows was sick. Daddy was careful not to sell milk from a sick cow. But there had never been a time when they had poured out all the milk at once. Never. She wasn't even sure how to do it. If they dumped it in the barnyard, it'd bring flies like the dickens.

Probably the best way was to pour it down the manure gutter. That would be easiest. Agnes clenched her hand around the phone receiver. The idea of throwing away perfectly good milk like it was cow manure made her feel almost sick.

It was like throwing away money. They needed every penny they could earn—even without the doctor's bill.

"Agnes?" The high voice cut into her thoughts.

"Yes, Mrs. Otto?"

"Dilly is doing just fine. I'm sure sorry about all this with your father."

"Thank you, Mrs. Otto."

"If I kept a car, I'd help out."

"Thank you, Mrs. Otto."

"Can you think of anyone else?"

Agnes shook her head, trying. "No. A car wouldn't really work anyway. Daddy built the back of the truck special to hold stacks of the crates."

There was a silence and Agnes listened to it for a few seconds. Then she drew in a deep breath. "Thank you, Mrs. Otto. If Mama calls again, tell her . . . " Agnes paused. She had been about to ask Mrs. Otto to tell Mama to come home as soon as she could—but it seemed like the wrong thing to do.

"I'll tell her you kids are all right."

"Thank you, Mrs. Otto," Agnes said again.

"Agnes? Are you all right?"

Agnes took a quick breath. No, she wasn't all right. She was sick with worry about everything. "Of course, Mrs. Otto," she said aloud. "Thank you for calling."

"You are very welcome," Mrs. Otto said politely. "Good evening to you, then."

Agnes settled the receiver back into the cradle and set the phone near the ringer box mounted on the wall. For a few seconds, she stood fingering the cord, running her hand over the shiny caps of the telephone bells. Then she turned around.

"What did she say?" Mary exploded. Charles stood beside her, his eyes eager for good news.

Agnes looked at them. "Mama has to take Daddy to Pueblo for an X-ray of his foot."

"What's an X-ray?" Mary asked, her voice tight and strained.

"It's like a picture of his bones," Agnes told her. "Mrs. Hanna taught us about it last year in school. It doesn't hurt," she added when she saw Charles's eyes go wide.

"Is something wrong with Daddy's bones?" His voice was tiny, barely audible.

"Doctor Lammee thinks the nail might have chipped them or something."

"The nail?" Charles echoed. "It chipped his bones?"

Agnes shook her head. "We don't know yet. Mama didn't sound too worried," she added, lying a little. Mama always sounded calm when things were terrible. "Mama said that the Pueblo X-ray machine takes better pictures than the one at the Lammees' hospital."

"What good does a picture do?" Mary demanded.

Agnes shrugged. "It helps the doctors see what's wrong." She stared at them, wishing she could think of something better to say. "We have a lot of work to do tonight," she said. She explained about the milk.

"On the *ground*?" Charles asked, his astonishment plain in the high, disbelieving tone of his voice. "Mama said to?"

Agnes nodded, wishing there was some other way around it.

"I hear the cows lowing," Mary said into the silence.

Agnes started down the hallway, aware that Mary and Charles had fallen in behind her like ducklings behind their mother. She led them outside, down the steps and across the barnyard.

The cows had finished their alfalfa hay and were ready to be let back into the high pasture for the night. They were milling around in front of the hayrick, switching their tails at the afternoon flies. The chickens were pecking up bits of spilled grain on the far side of the hayrick, sending up spurts of dirt and hay as they scratched.

Blaze whinnied from inside the barn and Agnes remembered she hadn't watered the horses yet today—it was usually one of her chores. Feeling guilty, she started toward the barn doors, then looked back over her shoulder. "Mary, would you open the pasture gate for the cows and run and check that the gate into the alfalfa pasture is locked tight? The last thing we need is bloated cows."

Mary nodded, then ran off downhill. Agnes watched her for a few seconds. The sun was getting low. The haystack in the middle of the field cast a long, lumpy shadow, joined grotesquely to the shadow of their old hay wagon. Agnes stared at it, an idea forming in her mind. Amazed that she hadn't thought of it before, Agnes smiled to herself. They could do it, and they would do it without Mr. Thomas's expensive help.

She turned around and looked at her brother. "Start turning the bottles in the crates," she told him, explaining her idea. "I'll be there in a second."

Charles nodded eagerly and ran off, and she could hear him singing to himself as he started to work. The idea of wasting the whole milking had been bothering him, too, she was sure. She thought about Mama and how hard it must have been for her to tell them to do it. It just seemed wrong.

Agnes hurried to water the horses and decided to give them a little extra grain. They were going to have to work for their supper tonight.

CHAPTER EIGHT

Agnes made quick work of feeding the horses, stopping only to let Blaze nuzzle her cheek, blowing a warm, hay-scented breath in her face. Then she hurried back outside. Mary was coming up from the bottom of the barnyard.

"I checked the gate. It's tight."

Agnes nodded. "Good. I have an idea."

"About dumping the milk?" Mary asked.

Agnes shook her head. "About how *not* to." Mary's eyes widened as she listened. They walked side by side along the barn, past the hayrick and the stacked bales, heading for the milk house.

Charles was still bent over the crate of clean jars stacked beside the steam table. The coal burner wasn't stoked now—there was no need. They picked up empties when they delivered, then washed them once they got home.

Agnes turned off the cooler and positioned a clean milk can beneath its steel faucet. She filled it half full. No point in chancing a spill trying to lift a full can. She poured the milk into the bottler tank, then filled the can halfway again. When she picked that one up, she gestured to Mary. "Get a second can. Only fill them half full."

By the time Agnes had poured the second half can into the bottler tank, Mary's was almost full enough. They traded cans, her empty for the half-full one Mary dragged toward her. Then Mary turned the spigot open wide while Agnes carried it on to the bottler. She dumped the milk into the tank, then turned back to find Mary pulling the next half-full can toward her.

Working together, it didn't take too long to empty the milk in the cooler into the bottler. Agnes stopped to catch her breath, then went to uncoil the boiler hose. She sprayed the inside of the cooler with scalding hot water, then added detergent. Taking the cleaning brush from its hook on the wall, she scrubbed at the stainless-steel tank, swirling the water hard.

Once she was finished washing, Agnes motioned to Mary to unplug the cooler tank drain. After the water ran out, Mary replaced the plug and ran to get the BK disinfectant from the shelf. Agnes added a half cup of it to the next wash, then they rinsed the tank with plain hot water. The odor of the disinfectant solution filled the milk house. Agnes smiled. The smell of the BK meant they were almost ready to start bottling. So far, so good. Maybe they were going to manage after all.

By the time she coiled the hose, Charles had the bottles turned over—almost four hundred of them. Mary set the first three crates on the bottler without being asked. Charles went around to the far side of the machine and checked the bin where the tube of flattened little paper caps fit.

She saw him reach in and she shouted over the noise. "Can you run the capper?"

Charles looked up, frowning. "I think so." He pulled out the little seat and positioned himself by the machine, one hand already on the lever.

Agnes nodded to Mary and raised her voice again. "Ready? Charles will cap. You can load empties and fill. I'll stack the finished crates by the door."

Mary nodded and she turned to flip the switch. The bottler came to life, its wheeled belts jiggling a little under the vibration of the motor. Agnes pulled up the lever that started the belts. Then, when the first crate of bottles was in place, she opened the valve that pumped the milk in the tank into the six tubes poised over the quart bottles in the crate.

The smooth columns of milk that came out of the machine filled the first crate of bottles in just a few seconds. The flow was cut off automatically when the bottles were filled within a half inch of the top. After a second's pause, the wheeled belt beneath the crate moved it forward toward the capper, bringing up another crate of empties that were stopped in place by a little metal bumper that had closed across the belt like a railroad gate.

Mary pulled the lever and the six streams of milk reappeared, filling the second batch of bottles. Then the little gate lifted and the crate moved toward Charles and the capper.

Agnes watched. Charles was still nudging the first crate into position, frowning, concentrating. Finally, he pulled the lever on his side of the machine and the capper lowered. The steel cup fittings lowered to push the paper over the glass bottle mouths, crushing each one of them into a perfect skin that doubled tightly under the edge, forming a tight seal.

As Agnes worked, stacking the full crates, she was careful not to clink the bottles against each other, or to set them down hard enough to chip the bottoms. She found herself worrying again, her thoughts bumping along in time with the clattery motor of the bottling machine.

Maybe it was wrong to disobey Mama. And what if she or Daddy called while they were out delivering? They'd have to worry for hours, wondering why no one was at the house. Agnes was sure that it would never occur to her parents that she and the kids would use the hay wagon to deliver milk.

Agnes swung the full, capped crates off the bottler

and set each one by the door, arranging them carefully. She didn't want to stack more than three high. Four crates stacked up were tippy. The only thing that would upset her parents more than wasted milk was wasted milk and broken bottles. Daddy warned them all about twenty times a week. Bottles were expensive to replace.

As Agnes carried another crate, she noticed that the caps were off center. They looked like they would hold, but the printing looked tilted. The outline of the Spanish peaks that formed the background behind the lettering was a little skewed. *Gleason Family Dairy* looked crooked.

"Hey!" she yelled at Charles, loud enough for him to hear her over the jingling clatter of bottles and machine. He looked up, startled. "The caps are crooked. Be more careful!"

He nodded, but the look that crossed his face was one of pure hurt. He had been concentrating on his work. Now, as he lowered his head, Agnes saw him biting his lip. She knew exactly how he felt. She felt that way far too often when Daddy scolded her. And Charles was trying so hard.

"It's just one crate," she hollered, trying to act like she had just noticed. "The rest look perfect!"

Charles looked up again, his face brightening.

Agnes smiled at him as she swung down another crate and added it to the stacks by the door. When the first three rows were three high, she started another set of rows. The bottler clacked and rattled and the rhythm of the engine started her thoughts spinning again as she worked.

Maybe she should call Mrs. Otto and tell her they were going to take the wagon on the milk route. But she knew that if she did, Mrs. Otto would discourage her, reminding her that she was supposed to obey her parents. Since she was fully intending to disobey them, the last thing she wanted was someone trying to talk her out of it. And Mrs. Otto might call Mr. Thomas to help them whether they wanted him or not. That would be her brand of kindhearted meddling.

Agnes counted the stacked crates. Forty-two. That meant eighteen to go. She glanced out the windows, trying to guess the time from the angle of the sunlight. They were better off than she had thought, she was pretty sure. She had been afraid that they would be so late delivering that all their evening customers would be finished with supper and halfway to bed.

She looked up to see Charles standing, fitting another tube of two hundred caps into the bin. He closed the lid carefully, nodding at her when he noticed her watching. She smiled at how earnest he looked. Was that how she looked when Daddy came to check on her work? But even Ralph had stopped whistling when he knew Daddy was watching him, she realized.

Agnes stacked another crate, careful to set it down gently. Daddy had been hardest of all on Ralph, now that she thought about it. He expected him to do things perfectly.

Agnes turned back for another crate, then another. As the machine clattered and vibrated, she tried to keep up. Finally, she noticed Mary standing still at the other end of the bottler. All the bottles had been filled. Charles had three more crates to cap and they would be finished. "Can you do stack, Mary? If you can, I'll get the cream out here."

Mary nodded, coming forward. "I think so. But Daddy never lets me lift the full ones."

Agnes stood aside. "See if you can."

Mary lifted down a full crate and walked with it to the stacks near the door. Slowly, carefully, she set it down. When she turned around, she nodded, smiling. "I'm fine."

Agnes turned. "I'll get the cream, then."

Agnes liked going into the cool room. In summer, it was the most wonderful temperature, mild and pleasant. In winter, it seemed just warm enough to be comfortable if she was wearing a thick jacket—which was Agnes's favorite kind of weather anyway. She undid the four latches and inhaled deeply as she opened the door. The cool room even smelled good.

Daddy had stuffed the walls with excelsior and old torn-up newspaper. He had tacked rubber stripping over the tiny crevices between the ceiling and the wall. There wasn't any place that the hot could get in, or the cold of winter.

Agnes brought out the crates of whipping cream first. It was so thick that when she tilted the bottles, it took several seconds for the cream to slant. The coffee cream was thinner, but it still looked delicious—Agnes realized how hungry she was.

The cream had been stacked four high with the crate handles turned out for Daddy to carry. Agnes managed three at a time. The pints were much lighter than the quarts of milk. Walking back and quickly, she finished stacking the cream crates just as Mary lifted the last quart bottles from the machine. Agnes flipped the switch and the jingling clatter stopped.

"Can you wash everything up?"

Mary nodded. So did Charles, but a little slower. He glanced out the barn doors toward the house. "After you do it," Agnes said, "go find something to eat to tide you over until supper. I'll go hitch up. And remember to bring the clipboard list," she added, looking at Mary.

Charles headed for the coiled hose. Mary followed him. Agnes watched them for a second or two before she turned away. At the horses' stall, she lay her cheek against Blaze's warm neck for a second and found unexpected tears flooding her eyes. She had been pretending to feel sure about everything for

Mary and Charles, but the truth was, she wasn't sure of anything at all.

Was Daddy going to be all right? Mama hadn't really said, had she? Blaze let her sniffle for about a minute, then began nuzzling her pockets for a carrot or an apple. Agnes had to smile. "That's all you care about? I should have known," she teased. Blaze rubbed her face against Agnes's shoulder, as though she was apologizing for being selfish. Agnes took a long, deep breath and dried her eyes, then went to get the harness.

Blaze stood like a rock, accepting the bit easily. Franklin was dancy, but not as bad as he was sometimes. Agnes got them both buckled into their collars and traces, then walked behind them, driving them into the yard, turning downhill to go out the pasture gates. Down by the haystack, she backed them up slowly, getting them straight on either side of the wagon tongue after two tries.

Once the harness was buckled up to the whiffletree, and the tongue fixed in place between the horses, Agnes climbed up on the driver's bench. After a moment, she shook the reins.

Franklin stepped off first, and Blaze kept pace. The wheels creaked and squealed on the first turn, then hushed. The harness jingled, and the late afternoon breeze brought the smell of green alfalfa from the lower pasture. If they were careful, they'd be all right.

CHAPTER NINE

The milk crates jingled and rattled as Agnes urged Blaze and Franklin up the steep drive. They weren't used to this. Only rarely did they go out the front gates, and Daddy never drove them all the way into town, except once or twice a year when he needed hay and the feed store delivery truck was broken down or something else went wrong.

"Should we stop and tell Mrs. Otto?" Mary asked in a small voice from her perch on the wagon bed.

Agnes clicked her tongue, shaking the reins, ignoring Mary's question. She had enough to think about right now without wondering about Mrs. Otto. The wagon was slanting as they went uphill toward Elder Street. "Anything sliding?" she asked over her shoulder.

"No," Mary answered in a sharp voice.

Agnes flipped the reins again, harder, stinging the horses' rumps just a little so they'd pull steady. The wagon creaked and jounced over the ruts at the top of the drive, then settled back to level as they came out onto the road.

"All okay?" Agnes called back, afraid to look.

"I think so," Mary answered. "The crates bounced, but I don't see any leaking or anything."

"My side is all right," Charles added.

"Did you hear what I asked about Mrs. Otto?" Mary wanted to know.

Agnes glanced over her shoulder. "No, I don't think we should tell Mrs. Otto, because if we do she'll try to talk us out of it or call Mr. Thomas and then Daddy will have to pay him. She knows we've hired him, just not *why*."

"But what if Mama calls and we don't answer?" Mary's voice was shrill, like she was about to cry.

Agnes nodded, turning far enough to meet Mary's eyes. "I thought of that. But what if Mrs. Otto answers and tells them what we're doing?"

"Mama might try to come home to help," Charles said.

"That's what I mean," Agnes said, craning around. "And the whole point is to do this on our own, right?"

"Right," Charles said instantly.

"Right," Mary said, a little slower.

"It'll take us a couple of hours," Agnes said, "maybe three. Then we'll be home. Chances are, Mama won't call until late anyway. She'll just figure we'll be outside at chores until dark, probably. We might have to do this twice. But Mrs. Otto said they would try to be home tomorrow night."

"Not tomorrow morning?" Charles asked, obviously surprised, and Agnes realized she had never really told them what Mrs. Otto had said.

"Maybe they'll find out Daddy is fine and be back sooner," she answered Charles, doing her best to keep her voice level and matter-of-fact. Just then, the right rear wheel sank into one of the ruts and the whole wagon jounced, slanting.

"Watch the crates!" Agnes shouted, pulling Franklin and Blaze to the left. The wagon lurched again as the wheel came up out of the rut, then flattened.

"Be more careful!" Mary called out, her voice high and peevish.

"I'm trying," Agnes said.

"You're not trying hard enough," Mary shot back.

"Do you want to drive the team?" Agnes snapped.

Mary was suddenly silent and Agnes turned to look at her. Her chin was high in the air, her posture stiff and stubborn.

"Do you?" Agnes demanded. "You can just take over everything right now, Mary Eileen Gleason."

"Maybe I should," Mary said, without looking at her.

Agnes checked the line the horses were taking between the ruts and set her hands against her knees to keep the reins even and steady. Then she turned around. "You've never even driven the wagon as far as the hayfield."

"Yes, I did, once."

"With Daddy sitting behind you with his hands on the reins?"

A car horn blared from ahead of them and Agnes jerked back around, staring at a Model A coming right at them. She pulled the team farther right and the wagon wheel went into the rut again as the car went by. It was Mr. Grosvek and he glared at them as he went past. The wagon dropped, then rose unevenly again, tilting its way up out of the rut. The bottles jangled in their steel-wire crates.

Agnes glanced over her shoulder. Mary was looking at her. She didn't look angry anymore, or stubborn. She just looked upset. "I'm sorry, Aggie. You're right, I can't drive the team any better than you can. Probably worse."

"Just stop arguing and look where you're going," Charles said, jabbing his finger toward the road ahead.

Agnes turned around in time to see another car coming. She pulled the horses to the right, giving the other driver practically the whole road. "I'm sorry, too," she called to Mary once it was past. The sound of the engine faded. The *clip-clop* of the horses' hooves was muffled by the dust.

"What if Daddy isn't all right," Mary said after a few seconds of silence. It wasn't a question, really, not one that expected an answer anyway. It sounded like she was talking to herself.

"He will be," Agnes answered anyway, trying to sound sure. Mary said nothing more.

The clopping of the horses' hooves deepened as they followed Elder Street past the last few farms and on into town where the road was harder packed. As the houses got closer together, the ruts were shallower, too, worn flat from the dozens of cars that passed every day.

At the white house with ivy on the chimney, Agnes pulled the team over as far right as she could get them without bumping the wheels up over the curb. Then she reined them to a stop. Franklin tossed his head and stamped a hoof. He was enjoying the adventure. Blaze just lowered her head to wait in her calm, patient way.

Agnes wrapped the reins on the brake handle and got down from the bench. "Mary, why don't you drive first? It's easy. You just move them up a house or two at a time. You can read the clipboard and tell us which houses are ours. Then, when Charles gets tired, you can take a turn delivering while he drives."

"I'm not going to get tired," Charles said.

"Have you ever helped deliver?" Agnes asked him. He shook his head. She tried to remember the first time Daddy had let her help. When she was nine? Charles was only seven.

"The milk bottles get heavy, Charles. Even Ralph gets tired."

He looked surprised again. "He told me it was easy."

Agnes shook her head. "He was just trying to show off. It's not. Ready? Driver keeps the list." She pulled the clipboard out from behind the seat. "If anyone wants extra, remember to tell whoever is driving so they can mark it off for Mama. The first six houses are ours, both sides. Charles, just go from one house to the next on your side. Leave full quarts for empties until you're out, then come get another crate. You have to come back for cream if someone wants it."

Mary climbed up onto the bench, unwrapping the reins. "I'll go really slow."

Agnes nodded and pulled a crate off the wagon. "Pull up about three houses at a time. That's what Daddy does. And keep checking the clipboard to tell us where to go next. The address numbers are in the first column."

The six quart bottles shivered and jiggled in rhythm with Agnes's steps as she walked toward the first house. It was the Castaglios' place. They had five kids and they always took five quarts, morning and evening. Mrs. Castaglio met her at the door.

"By wagon this evening?" she said, looking out toward the curb.

"Yes, ma'am," Agnes answered, trying to sound cheerful and polite like Daddy always did.

"And where is your father?" she asked.

Agnes climbed the porch steps, the crate braced against her chest, unsure what to say. She didn't think Daddy would want the whole town to know about his injury. Not that anyone would think any less of him for it, but he might feel silly about stepping on a nail in his own barnyard.

"Daddy will be back by tomorrow," Agnes said politely. Mrs. Castaglio smiled. "That's good. I need five quarts tonight. And two pints whipping cream. I'm making a bread pudding."

Agnes set five quarts of milk into the milk box nailed to the porch railing, then picked up the five empties that Mrs. Castaglio had put out beneath it. She always washed out her bottles clear as crystal so there was no sour smell.

"I'll go get your cream," Agnes told her, looking up to see Charles across the street. He was standing on the grass in front of the Greens' house, looking up at Mr. Green standing on the porch steps.

Agnes hurried to the wagon and set her crate back on, leaving it close to the edge where she could pull out the extra quart as soon as she had room in the next crate. Then, she climbed up onto the wagon bed to reach two pints of cream from the cream stacks in the middle of the wagon. "Five quarts as usual and two pints whipping cream," she told Mary. Moving carefully, making sure that she didn't drop the pints, she walked as fast as she could to Mrs. Castaglio's milk box and set the cream beside the milk. Mrs. Castaglio had gone inside. Agnes whirled and ran back to the wagon.

Charles was heading straight for the next house. From the way he was walking, the first customers hadn't taken more than one or two quarts. His crate still looked heavy.

Agnes grabbed another crate, laying her one left-over quart slantwise between the first and second rows. She jiggled it lightly. The cap held. She knew Daddy would holler at her for carrying the extra quart on its side, but they had to hurry.

Agnes looked at the sun. It was getting lower—it was probably about five now. "The list says Mrs. Ensign usually takes one quart," Mary said, gesturing to the next house.

Agnes hurried up the stepping-stones that formed the front walk. There was no milk box and only one empty sitting beside the door. She set her extra quart down and picked the empty up. Turning to go to the next house, she cut across the yard.

Daddy wouldn't like that, either, but there were no flower beds, just the grass, and she didn't think anyone would mind.

The next house took three quarts of milk and the woman sent her running back to the wagon for three pints of cream, two coffee, one whipping. Agnes rearranged the bottles in her crate, taking out the empties and consolidating them, then looked across the street. Charles was one house back. She glanced up at Mary, who sat holding the reins, watching Charles, too. "Help him any way you can." Mary nodded as Agnes turned away, carrying the cream and more milk.

The customer met her out in front, taking the cream with a cordial smile.

"Your daddy too busy at home to deliver today?"

"He'll be back by tomorrow," Agnes said, realizing that people were probably asking Charles the same question.

Agnes carried milk to the next house as Mary moved the wagon up. On the way back, she saw Charles starting away from the wagon. Mary was sliding a crate around, arranging them closer to the edge of the wagon bed for Charles.

"Charles?" Agnes called.

He slowed and turned. "What?"

Agnes walked closer, motioning to Mary to listen, too. "Don't tell anyone Daddy is hurt," she said quietly once she was close enough. "If anyone asks, just say he'll be back tomorrow."

They both nodded, but Charles wrinkled his forehead. "I already told one man. The second house."

Agnes nodded. "Just don't tell anyone else."

Mary was frowning. "Why?"

Agnes shrugged. "Daddy just wouldn't want us to."

"Did Mama say not to?"

Agnes shook her head. "I'm not sure why, exactly. But you know how Daddy hates for anyone to know his business."

Charles set down his crate, then straightened, rubbing his arms. "People might think about changing to another dairy if they thought it was just a bunch of kids from now on."

Agnes looked at him. "I hadn't even thought of that."

"All right," Mary said impatiently. "So we won't tell." She was eyeing the untouched stacks of crates on the wagon. "How many houses do we have to do?"

Agnes had been hoping that neither one of them would ask that question. She had been trying not to think about it. "It's about ninety families, Mama told me once."

"Ninety houses," Mary repeated. "*Ninety*?"

Agnes nodded. "But it'll go quicker than you think."

"Not if we just stand here talking," Charles said.

Agnes nodded. He was right. She set her crate of empties on the wagon and climbed up to unload a full one. "Mary?"

Her sister stopped mid-step and looked back. "Once you move the wagon up, you can hand us the full ones and take the empties so we can stop climbing up and down."

Mary nodded, then turned again. Agnes glanced at Charles. He was struggling to walk fast with the crate clutched against his belly. How were they ever going to make it before dark? Maybe this had been a bad idea after all.

CHAPTER TEN

Agnes was getting tired. They were on Cedar Street now though, nearly all the way down to Main—almost finished. As she walked back toward the wagon for more quarts of milk, Mary was busily rearranging crates. She saw Agnes coming and slid a full one toward her.

Suddenly, there was a clatter, the sound of a wire crate hitting a cobbled walk, then the smash of breaking glass. Agnes pushed the full crate back onto the wagon bed as she and Mary both looked up. A second later, they were both running. Agnes was faster and she pounded up the walk, Mary not far behind her.

Charles was lying on the cobblestone walk, his back to Agnes. She danced to a stop, taking in the shattered glass, the spilled milk. Mary came up behind her as Charles sat up. He held up his hand. There was a little blood in the center of his palm. He brushed at it, staring at the cut. Then he looked up at Agnes, his eyes round and wide.

"It isn't even deep, Agnes. Don't cry."

"I'm not," she said quickly, but she wiped at her eyes. She had imagined him cut badly and it had scared her.

"I broke two, Aggie," Charles was saying sadly. "I'm sorry."

"I broke three once," she said, to make him feel better. "And Daddy broke a whole crate's worth one morning when I was with him in the truck. He pulled one crate out and the wire bottom got snagged on the crate below it."

"You all right out there?" a woman was calling from the screen door.

"Yes, ma'am," Agnes answered, then cleared her throat and wiped at her eyes. "Could we borrow a broom and put the glass in your trash, please?" She turned around and bumped into Mary. "You and Charles finish these houses while I clean up, all right?"

Mary nodded. She glanced back toward the wagon, looking worried. "He's fine," Agnes reassured her, but Mary was shaking her head, looking toward the street. In that instant, Agnes understood. They had run without thinking, leaving the reins slack on the horses' backs. Franklin was tossing his head and sidling forward an uncertain step or two, pulling Blaze with him.

"Whoa up," Agnes shouted, sprinting toward the wagon. "Whoa, Blaze!"

As she ran she saw Franklin ducking his head, extending his neck, then raising his muzzle, pulling more slack into the reins. He walked forward and Agnes slowed instantly, afraid of startling him into a trot.

"Whoa now, please," she breathed as Mary raced past her, shouting and waving her arms. Franklin saw her coming and danced into a jog. Blaze let him move her along, shaking her head at the unfamiliar absence of pressure on the reins.

"Mary!" Agnes shouted, but it was too late. Franklin threw up his head and snorted, shying to one side. Startled, Blaze picked up her pace, her eyes rolling back as she tried to see the danger Franklin had seen.

"Stop, Mary!" Agnes shouted. "Stop it, you're just scaring them!"

Mary slid to a halt and Agnes looked around, trying to figure out what to do. They were headed toward Main Street—with less than half a block to go. If the horses got out into the cars and traffic, no telling where they would end up or what would happen. She could see the milk crates jouncing now, if they broke into a gallop, everything was going to end up broken and bent.

Agnes felt sick imagining Daddy's face if that happened. They could never replace all the bottles and crates at once—it'd be enough to put them out of business the way things were now. She struggled against panic, hating the hard times. Everything always seemed to come down to money. Everything that went wrong was worse because of whatever money it cost. The hospital, the broken bottles . . .

Agnes jogged along, following the horses, calling to them to calm down, to slow down. She looked down the block, hoping someone would be out on a front stoop, see the loose team, and walk out to stop them. It wouldn't be that hard as long as they were just trotting like this, but someone had to stand in front of them, not come racing up from behind. As Franklin rose into a faster trot, Agnes ran along the edges of the yards, jumping bushes and flower beds.

Mary was yelling from somewhere behind her, but Agnes didn't dare look back. One stumble and the horses would be too far ahead, uncatchable. Franklin was still tossing his head, still excited by the slack reins.

At the corner of Main Street, Franklin slowed just a little and Agnes sprinted, hoping they would stop, but they didn't. Franklin stepped right out into the roadway, Blaze a reluctant, wild-eyed partner.

One car honked and swerved, but it went on. Agnes rounded the corner about fifty feet behind the wagon and looked down the street. There were no cars coming now and Franklin was trotting faster, his head high like a frisky colt.

Agnes kept running, desperate and breathing hard. Here on Main Street, the pavement was smooth enough to keep the crates from rattling their way off the wagon, but if the horses swerved and got one wheel up on the curb, or if the wagon tilted or over-turned, every bottle on it would break—and the horses could get hurt, too.

A barking dog suddenly raced out of a yard a lit-tle ways in front of the horses. Agnes saw Franklin break stride as the dog ran snarling toward him. Blaze was balking, holding him back. The dog was loud, bounding to a stiff-legged stop in front of the horses. It lowered its head, sniffing, and the horses came to an uneasy standstill. Agnes raced alongside the wagon, her eyes on the dragging reins.

Just then, someone whistled at the dog and it whirled, running toward its yard. The wagon began to roll again as Franklin broke back into a trot, pulling the startled Blaze with him. Agnes ran, her lungs aching and her legs heavy. She saw the wagon sliding past and knew she would never reach the reins. Abruptly, she veered and managed to jump halfway on the wagon, her belly on the bed, her legs dangling over the side, dangerously close to the spinning spokes of the front wheel. Franklin threw his head up and snorted, startled by the blur of motion in the cor-ner of his eye. He rose into a spanking trot again, turning his head one way, then the other. Blaze was scared now, too. Her eyes were ringed in white. Frightened, and spooking each other with their snorting and head tossing, they broke into a canter, then pounded into a full gallop.

The edge of the wagon bed grated against Agnes's ribs as she struggled not to fall beneath the wagon. She imagined the crushing pressure of the rear wheel and dug her fingernails into the rough planks. Dragging herself forward inch by inch, Agnes heard someone shout, but she had no ability to understand, much less answer. Finally, when her hipbones were along the edge of the wagon bed, her balance changed and she found she could swing her right leg up, hooking her knee over the edge. She clawed forward again, managing to roll onto the wagon.

For a few seconds she lay still, imagining the spinning wheel, beneath her now, where it belonged. Then she got to her knees, balancing herself as the galloping horses started down the long, gradual incline toward the center of town. The crates were jittering, but not sliding—the road was still smooth and flat. She walked forward on her knees, her eyes fixed on the flying manes and tails of the horses. The reins were loose across their backs, the ends invisible, dragging the ground beneath the wagon.

Slowly, gripping the back of the driver's bench so tightly her knuckles were white, Agnes crawled over, glancing at the roadway ahead. There were cars farther down, toward Seventh Street and the center of town, but no one was coming up this way. Steadying herself, Agnes kept one hand on the back of the driver's bench and leaned out, trying to catch the loop of rein that sagged from its guide ring on Franklin's bellyband. She couldn't.

Trembling, Agnes slid down and crouched on the footrest, hanging onto the edge of the seat this time, and tried again. Reaching downward, acutely aware of the pounding hooves that were so close, she got one finger beneath the rein and managed to coax it into her hand. Quickly, she straightened, pushing herself back into the driver's bench, letting the rein slide through two fingers, but keeping hold of it. She sat a moment, then wrapped the rein around the brake handle and started over.

The second one was easier. When she was holding both of Franklin's reins, Agnes looked up again. She still had five or six blocks before she came into midtown traffic. She began to hope. But she knew that hauling back on Franklin's reins was foolhardy. The wagon could swerve if Blaze kept going—maybe sharply enough to turn over, or tangle the horses in an awful accident. They weren't surefooted on pavement. Agnes sat still for a moment, breathing hard.

"Hey!"

The voice was close and Agnes looked up in time to see a startled older man step back abruptly, a newspaper clutched in his hand. She shuddered. If the horses ran someone down . . . She wrapped Franklin's second rein around the brake and crouched on the footrest again.

She leaned out, but it was impossible. Blaze's reins had sagged into loops that dragged the ground. Heart pounding, Agnes sat back up, looking around, thinking frantically. Her eye fell on the whip, standing upright in its holder. Daring to hope again, she grabbed it, then crouched on the footrest once more.

Holding on with one hand while she leaned out and down, Agnes reached toward the outside rein first, extending the whip, careful not to jab it into the pavement—then she would drop it. Trying not to look down at the hard black pavement and the heavy hooves thundering along it, Agnes leaned farther, holding her breath as she slid the whip beneath the rein. She hooked it and lifted the tip slowly, carefully letting the rein slide along it as she pulled it toward herself. It seemed to take forever as she listened to the galloping hoofbeats, the pavement a rushing blur only a few feet away. Once the rein was finally in her hand, she scooted back, laying the whip on the seat as she looked up.

About half a block in front of her, people were crossing the street, laughing and talking. The group included two little children, walking a few steps ahead of the others. Agnes shouted at them as she jerked

Franklin's reins from the brake handle. Then she hauled back on all three reins, hoping that Blaze would have the sense to slow even if the pull was uneven.

The people heard her shout and scurried back to the curb. Grabbing the little children, a man yelled at Agnes as the wagon thundered past. She glanced back to see him shaking his fist in the air.

"Whoa, you fools," she yelled at the horses. "Whoa up!" She jerked the reins, hard, then kept up her steady pull again. Blaze tipped an ear backward. She slowed a little, forcing Franklin to come in hand along with her. Agnes anchored the reins around her waist and used her legs to shove herself backward in the seat, increasing the pressure relentlessly. Blaze came back into a collected canter, again forcing Franklin to slow with her. He tossed his head and fought the reins, dragging Agnes almost back into a standing position before he ducked his muzzle and gave in.

When Blaze dropped back to a trot, Agnes knew she had won. She fought with Franklin another few strides, until he finally broke his canter and began to trot, too, sides heaving. Once she had them down to a walk, Agnes risked a look backward. Two crates had rattled perilously close to the edge, but not a single bottle had broken.

Daddy and Mama would be furious when someone told them about this—and someone would be sure to.

At least half a dozen people had seen her, and someone would figure out who she was from the milk crates on the wagon. But at least no harm had been done. Agnes turned the team around in a wide half circle, watching carefully for cars, and started back to where Mary and Charles would be waiting. Her hands were shaking and her heart felt like it would never slow down again. Daddy would be furious.

Agnes was almost all the way back up to Cedar Street before she stopped trembling. Turning back onto it, she had to jiggle the reins hard to get the horses to hurry along a little. They were tired now.

"Fool horses," she muttered at them again, but she knew she was really upset with herself. Horses couldn't be expected to stand forever without being tethered. It was their nature to graze, to walk around. And if something scared them, it was their instinct to take off at a gallop.

"Oh, you did it!" Agnes heard Mary shout as she turned back down Cedar Street. Her voice was high and squeaky with relief and excitement.

"I knew you would stop them," Charles called. His hand was wrapped in a white bandage now. They were standing on the lawn of the house where he had fallen, close to the curb. The woman of the house stood back a little farther, a broom in her hand.

"We have all just been hoping and praying," she said. "My husband has the car and I can't drive anyway—and then after just a few minutes, we really weren't sure which way to send someone . . . I was about to call the police, though. I had begun to think we had better do at least that much."

"It's all right," Agnes said, mostly to make her stop her breathless talking. Everything *was* all right, so long as Charles really wasn't hurt. She pulled the team to a stop and got down out of the wagon. Her knees were still rubbery and shaky as she shoved the two crates that had gotten close to the edge back toward the center of the wagon bed. Then she looked at Charles again.

He took a few quick steps toward her, leaning forward to whisper. "She wanted to wrap it up like this so I let her, but it isn't deep at all."

"Well, we had better finish the route now, ma'am," he said, turning. "We appreciate your help, and I am awful sorry if you find any bits of broken glass in your yard. I tried to get it all up."

"Oh, don't you worry about that even for a second," the woman said, obviously charmed. She suddenly laughed quietly.

Agnes looked at her. "What?"

"I wonder if the whipping cream is already whipped."

For a second, Agnes thought she meant it and started toward the wagon to look. Then she heard Charles laughing.

"Maybe not whipped," the woman said, smiling, "but it could be halfway to butter from all the shaking."

"We'd better go now, ma'am," Mary said in a polite voice, and Agnes was glad. She didn't feel like laughing at anyone's jokes.

"I'll turn the wagon around," Agnes said, wanting more than anything to be finished, to be on the way home. They only had about ten more houses do to.

Mary and Charles walked along the side of the street, waiting until the wagon was back in position. "I'll carry for a while. You rest," Mary said. "We've just been standing around listening to that lady talk." She whispered the last few words so that the woman, still standing on her porch, couldn't hear. "Now, tell us what happened."

Agnes gave them a quick description of what she had had to do to stop the team. Charles whistled and Mary's eyes went wide. "Maybe we should have worried more."

Agnes shook her head. "Let's just get finished."

Mary nodded and Charles crawled up to push two crates of full quarts to the edge of the wagon. Agnes sank down on the hard wood, one hand firmly on the reins, and pulled the clipboard from its place behind the back of the driver's bench.

CHAPTER ELEVEN

Going up the last little rise in Elder Street, Agnes began to feel better. They hadn't done so badly after all. They had delivered the milk instead of throwing it away, and even though things had gone wrong, they had turned out all right. And it was dusky, but it wasn't dark out yet.

"I just hope Mama hasn't called yet," Mary said as they put the horses away.

"Charles, why don't you go on up to the house while Mary and I finish up," Agnes said. She glanced at Mary. "Is that all right? Then, if she does call, he can answer."

Mary nodded. "I'll start washing if you can unload. My arms feel like they are going to drop off."

Agnes nodded. "It's not much longer, Mary, and we can all go to bed."

Agnes unhitched by the milk house, leaving the still-loaded wagon standing there while she led the horses into the barn. She hayed them and refilled their water bucket. She patted Blaze and stuck her tongue out at Franklin. "Good night," she told them. "See you in the morning."

"Agnes?" It was Mary, calling from the door. "I've got the boiler stoked and running," she said, coming in.

"Good," Agnes said, turning quickly. "Let's get to it, then. I can't wait to eat something and get to bed."

"Bed," Mary said as they went out the door. She said the word like it meant something wondrous, magical.

Agnes pushed the barn doors closed and slid the bar across. They always locked the barn at night, to keep at least some of the rats out of the grain and the coyotes away from the two old hens that roosted inside instead of in the chicken coop.

Agnes turned toward the milk house and Mary fell into step beside her. Mary had turned the milk house light on, Agnes saw as they got closer, even though it wasn't quite dark yet. If Daddy had been there, she would have gotten a scolding for that, Agnes was sure. Daddy hated for them to waste a penny's worth of anything.

Agnes looked at the position of the wagon and smiled. She had pulled it in close and straight, just the right distance from the door to make unloading as easy as it could ever be. While Mary went inside, Agnes got the single case of cream they hadn't sold, then followed, carrying it in to the cool room. If they could sell it first thing in the morning, it'd be all right. If not, she would have to throw it away. Daddy hated to throw away cream, she knew, but she wasn't going to have time to make butter before it soured—not if they had to deliver using the wagon again.

The idea of starting the long chores over in the morning made Agnes sigh. She pushed the thought away. "One thing at a time," she said aloud, and began unloading the wagon. It was easier than loading it had been. She could carry three crates of empties at a time.

As Mary filled the wash tank with hot water and detergent, Agnes realized how weary she was and felt herself getting angry at Ralph again. He had just walked away when they needed him most. They had managed tonight, but what about tomorrow and the day after that, if Daddy was too hurt to work right away? Even with Mama helping, it'd be too much. And when school started, things would only get worse. Maybe she would have to quit school to help at home. She wouldn't miss Mrs. Wright's long history lectures, but she would miss arithmetic and reading. And her friends.

The sound of the electric brush on the washer startled Agnes as she came back through the door with more empties. Mary was starting the bottles. She looked tired as she pushed her hair back from her face, but she smiled. Agnes could see her lips moving and knew Mary was singing quietly, hiding her voice in the noise of the brush motor. She would be slow, but she wouldn't stop. Daddy was the fastest bottle washer. Without him here, this was going to take quite a while. But, Agnes realized, without Daddy here to get impatient with Mary, there would be no arguments, no tears.

Agnes tried to hurry, carrying four crates instead of three at a time, walking a little faster—but still careful. They had had enough close calls for one day. And, she admitted to herself, glancing toward the door, she didn't want to give Daddy anything else to get upset about. She knew she would catch heck for the runaway and for the broken bottles. Oh, how she longed for Ralph to come home. If he had been here, Daddy would have given *him* the lecture, while she and Mary and Charles had skipped off to bed. As it was, she was going to have to do everything, decide everything, and get scolded for anything that went wrong.

Agnes paused, going back over her own thoughts. How often had Ralph felt like she was feeling right now? She was tired, and sore and hungry, and dreading Daddy's arrival. As much as she wanted to see that he was all right, she didn't want to listen to him find fault in everything they had tried to do to help. Agnes shook her head and forced herself to concentrate on working.

After the empties were all in, Agnes realized

Mary was washing bottles faster than she ever had. Wearing the heavy rubber gloves that protected her hands from the scalding water and gave her a grip on the soapy glass, she stayed bent over the brush, working steadily. Agnes stopped to watch her fit a bottle over the spinning brush, letting the bristles scour the glass. Then she set the clean quart container in a crate and reached for a dirty one, all in the same motion.

Agnes finished unloading, then slid the crates of clean bottles to one side of the metal-topped table, making room for more as Mary worked. When the time came to rinse them in the BK solution, Agnes had the second tank filled before Mary was ready. Then she started the boiler beneath the steam table.

Mary started putting the washed bottles through the disinfectant rinse. Each crate was lowered in, left for about thirty seconds, then hoisted out again, streaming water, and set back on the metal table. Agnes fell to work beside her and they worked as Mama and Daddy usually did, taking turns at the tank. Whoever was not waiting the few seconds while the disinfectant worked was getting another crate from the table and walking back.

The clear rinse went fastest of all because the tank was biggest. Agnes and Mary took two crates at once and it wasn't long before most of the bottles were rinsed.

"I'll start loading the steam table," Mary said. "I bet Charles fell asleep," she added, gesturing toward the house with her chin as she lifted a crate of rinsed bottles, tilting it to let the water run out faster.

"You're probably right," Agnes answered over the noise, feeling a little guilty that she hadn't even thought about Charles for an hour. It was strange to think that Mama was not in the kitchen, keeping supper hot until they made it in.

"Charles worked hard the whole time, didn't he?" Mary shouted over the rumbling of the boiler. She was smiling.

"He sure did," Agnes said, then nodded in case Mary couldn't hear her over the machines.

Mary's smile widened. "And you stopped the team from running away. You must have looked like a cowboy in a movie!"

Agnes smiled, watching as Mary turned to go back to work. She had stopped the team, all right. But Daddy was going to be upset because she had let them get away in the first place. She felt her smile dissolve. The more she thought about it, the more she wondered if they should try to deliver in the morning. Maybe they should just play it safe and dump the milk if Daddy wasn't there to help.

Once the last of the bottles had been through the clear rinse, Agnes pitched in at the steam table, taking off the sterilized bottles every seven minutes while Mary loaded more from the other side. They finally finished and turned off all the equipment and washed down the floors and backsplashes with BK solution.

When Mary turned the hose off, the silence was strange and unsettling in Agnes's ears. Somewhere, in the back corner by the cool room door, a cricket chirped. Outside, one of the cows lowed quietly in the pasture.

As Agnes led the way toward the porch, she pulled in long, cool breaths that seemed to settle all the way to her feet before she let them out. The night was perfect, warm and quiet. The moon was up and the stars had come out.

The kitchen light was on and the back door stood open. Looking down the long hall as she opened the door, Agnes was astounded by the smell of cooking that enveloped her. Her stomach clenched and she realized how incredibly hungry she was. With Mary at her heels, she turned into the kitchen and saw Charles standing next to the stove.

"Mama had some leftover chicken in the ice box, but it wasn't enough. So I mixed it with some gravy and boiled up onions and carrots to put in and I—"

"And you are the most wonderful little brother in the world." Mary said it flatly, and it made them all laugh.

Agnes had to swallow before she could speak, her

mouth was watering so. "We thought you were asleep."

Charles shrugged. "I almost was, on the couch. But then I was too hungry and I knew you would be, too. Mama called," he admitted in a lower voice. "That's what woke me up. She said Daddy splintered some little bones, but he's all right. They'll be home tomorrow night." He stirred at the pot on the stove. "I didn't tell her we delivered. I thought it'd make a better surprise and that way she couldn't say not to in the morning."

"Daddy's all right?" Mary asked.

Charles nodded. "I think he will be. Mama said he would."

Agnes nodded, taking it in. Her parents were not coming home tonight. The responsibility for the morning milking and the decision to deliver or not were all hers, whether she wanted them or not.

Wearily, she went upstairs with Mary a half step behind her. They washed up and changed into clean clothes. Agnes put her yellow dress back on. Mary wore last year's dress of blue and pink flowered floursack cotton. They would need to wash clothes soon. Tomorrow, if they didn't deliver, they could manage a laundry. "Once Mama and Daddy get home we can catch up on other chores," she said, thinking aloud.

"Oh, my gosh," Charles said suddenly.

"What?" Agnes asked.

"I didn't feed the pigs at all today." He looked

frantic. That's my regular chore. How could I forget to do it?"

Mary's eyes were wide. "I never grained the chickens, either."

"And we need to shut the coop for the night," Agnes added. She looked longingly at the stew on the stove, then motioned them toward the door. "I'll light the lantern and we can go finish things up before we eat."

Groaning, Charles nodded. They filed across the porch and out to the barn, Charles carrying the scrap tin Mama kept on the sink. By the time they came back in, Agnes could hear her stomach rumbling.

They sat at the table while Charles fussed with bowls and the ladle. He was a little awkward with both—he almost never helped in the kitchen. But he wouldn't let either of them help. Once he had the stew served, he sat down, smiling broadly. Agnes noticed that his bowl was less full and pointed at it, raising her eyebrows. "You said you were hungry, didn't you?"

He nodded and ducked his head. "I already ate some. I couldn't wait."

"You are still the best brother in the world," Mary said in a serious voice. This time no one laughed. They were all spooning stew into their mouths. It was scorched a little; Agnes could taste a burned flavor. It was the best stew she had ever eaten.

CHAPTER TWELVE

At three-thirty, when her alarm clock began to ring, Agnes jackknifed in her bed, bolting straight up, fumbling with the clock to silence the sound. Her heart slammed against her ribs and she was conscious of the feeling that something was terribly wrong. In that instant, she remembered Daddy and Mama weren't there, and why—

Outside, the rooster crowed. Mary didn't move. They were all so used to the rooster singing up the sun that he rarely woke anyone but Daddy, who used him as an alarm clock. Agnes lay still staring at the shadows that hid the ceiling. She wondered what it would be like to awaken to the sounds of a city, of traffic and voices and the hum of factories. Was that the kind of place Ralph would end up?

Agnes counted to fifty. The rooster crowed three more times, and Mary only turned over, sighing in her sleep. Agnes slid her legs to the side, rolling into a sitting position, watching her sister. Mary did not move.

Agnes stood up, smoothing the dress she had not meant to fall asleep in. It was wrinkled and it would look like she had slept in it, but there wasn't much she could do about that now. Her only other dress was filthy. Maybe she could manage to do some wash after they delivered. She hated to be such a mess when Daddy came home.

Padding barefoot on the cold floor, Agnes slipped through the door, then closed it behind herself, turning the glass knob slowly to make the catch click a little less loudly than usual. Once it was shut, she stood still a few seconds longer, listening. There was no sound from within the room. Mary was asleep.

Agnes tiptoed down the hall and peeked into Charles's room. He had started sleeping with the door open a crack when Ralph left, partly to let in a little light from the living room below, she was sure, and the sound of the radio or Mama and Daddy talking downstairs. Agnes could see him curled up beneath his blankets, still as could be.

Agnes started down the stairs. The planks creaked and she went slowly. By the time she stepped off the staircase onto the smooth wood of the front room floor, she was shivering, as much from nervousness as from the chilly night air. She wasn't at all sure what she should do and she wanted to decide before Mary and Charles got up.

Slipping out the back door, Agnes glanced up at

the sky. The moon was down. And the horizon to the east was graying already—even though it was still dark out. She thought about lighting the lantern that hung just inside the door but decided not to. She could hardly get lost between here and the barn, and it wasn't really snake weather yet.

Agnes squared her shoulders. She would just go put the grain in the stanchions, feed the horses, then come back and start breakfast. All the while, she could think, and once she had decided what to do, she would waken Mary and Charles.

Crossing the barnyard to the milk house, Agnes heard the rooster crow twice more. Silly old bird. Did he really believe that the sun wouldn't come up without him? Agnes lifted the lock bar and slid it backward, then opened the barn door. The sharp squeal of the hinges seemed to almost echo.

Blaze whickered at her.

"Good morning, silly mare," Agnes said softly, wishing she had brought the lantern after all. The inside of the barn was pitch black. Daddy was usually the first one out, she realized, and he always carried a lantern.

Blaze whickered again as Agnes came into the dark barn, leaving the doors standing wide to let in the dim predawn light from outside. Agnes walked barefoot through the dust and the powdery bits of hay, feeling around for the bucket, then the grain sack, reaching inside it for the coffee can. She counted the canfuls and then set the bucket near the door. The far end of the barn was too dark to fill the stanchion feed-boxes now. She grained the horses, patting Blaze's neck.

"You had better behave when we are in town this morning," she said to Franklin, then realized what she had said.

Agnes stood very still. Had she really decided that easily? It would be a lot easier to just do what Mama had said on the phone; dump the milk. Then Daddy couldn't fault her for anything beyond what had already happened. But it felt wrong to waste the milk, especially now, when she knew they could deliver on their own if they had to. And the morning route was shorter. Most of their customers preferred evening deliveries. Somehow, not delivering felt a lot like what Ralph had done. It felt like running away.

Besides, Agnes told herself, Daddy was going to be upset about so many things already that a few more might not make all that much difference. She smiled wryly, listening to the horses eat their grain, grinding it in rhythmic, circular motions, their jaws working steadily. She felt her way to the open bale of hay and hoisted a flake into the hayrick. Then she spun around and ran toward the house. Now that she had decided, they had to get going.

It was still almost pitch dark inside the house.

Agnes turned on the kitchen light and blinked, her eyes stinging from the sudden brightness. She set about making pancake batter. Maybe if they ate a big breakfast, they wouldn't get too hungry before deliveries were finished.

Agnes leaned close to the window, cupping her hands around her face to shut out the glare of the electric light. The sky was graying in the east, but it was impossible to tell if it was cloudy or clear yet. She hoped the weather would be good again.

Agnes heard footsteps on the planked floor in the hall and looked up to see Charles reflected in the window. He was dressed and squinting in the light. "Should I go wake Mary?"

Agnes nodded. "And tell her we'll have pancakes this morning," she said, turning away from the chilly glass to face him.

"Pancakes?" Charles echoed. There was pure delight in his voice.

Agnes smiled at him. "Go tell her. And hurry. We have a lot to do this morning."

The pancakes came out fluffy and good. Agnes ate her own standing up, minding the skillet as she cooked. By the time she was finished, Mary and Charles were standing up to take their plates to the sink. They all cleaned up, with Mary washing the dishes without being asked.

"I'll go let the cows in," Charles said from the

doorway. "I'll light a lantern." He added the last sentence in a tentative voice. Daddy never let him carry lanterns, much less light them.

"Be careful with it," Agnes told him.

He ran to the front room to get a match from the hearth. She heard him dragging a chair and realized he couldn't reach the lantern. She started to go help him, then stopped herself. He was managing his own way and there was plenty to do without hovering over him.

While Agnes tidied the room, pushing in their chairs and wiping the table, Mary put the milk pitcher away, and the jar of honey. In seconds, the kitchen was restored to order, the butter dish back in the cupboard and the crumbs all in the scrap tin for the pigs.

Agnes ran outside to open the chicken coop. The rooster strutted out, clucking his wives into following him out into the dusky morning. The sky was pink to the east now.

The screen door banged open and Charles came out with the lantern, carrying it high. Agnes watched him walk toward the barn, Mary at his heels. They wouldn't need the lantern for more than fifteen or twenty more minutes, really, and Agnes knew that Daddy would call it a waste, but Charles was proud of having lit it and she wasn't about to say anything to him about it.

Agnes looked at the sky again. For all her hurrying,

they were getting a late start again. But at least they had had breakfast and a night's sleep.

"I left the grain bucket full with the can in it," Agnes called out. "I just want to get my shoes on."

"We'll get started milking," Mary called back to her.

Agnes went up the porch steps, smiling to herself. Mary had sounded like Mama and Charles had looked so earnest, carrying the lantern. They were both doing everything they possibly could to help and she loved them for it. She would never argue with Mary again, she promised herself. And Charles deserved to never be teased or tricked again.

Running up the hall and turning to go up the stairs, Agnes wished Ralph could have seen Charles marching along holding the lantern practically over his head. Where was he, she wondered for the hundredth time. Was he sleeping in some train yard with other men looking for work? Was he cold and hungry?

Agnes perched on the side of her bed to pull on her socks, then pushed her feet into her shoes. As she stood up, she noticed a sore muscle in her shoulder and stretched. Both shoulders were sore—probably from carrying crates. She started for the stairs.

Milking went slowly—or so it seemed to Agnes. They walked the half-full cans of milk to the cooler again and every time they went, the sun seemed a lot higher in the sky. The separator seemed to go too slow and the capper on the bottler jammed twice. Charles had to throw away ten or twenty caps and Agnes saw him putting an empty BK container over them in the rubbish can so Daddy wouldn't see. Even the loading seemed to take too long. By the time they had the horses hitched up, the sun was bright and hot and halfway overhead.

"I want to put a sweater on," Agnes said as Mary and Charles came out of the milk house. She could smell disinfectant on their hands from washing up the bottler and the cans.

"It's too hot for a sweater," Mary said.

Agnes pointed at the wrinkles in her dress. "It'll look a little better than this, though."

Mary nodded. "We'll walk the wagon around to the gate."

Agnes started for the house, going in the back door at a run, swinging herself around the bottom of the bannister and taking the stairs two at a time. In her room she pulled a school sweater out of her trunk and put it on. Then, as she turned back toward her door, the sound of a truck engine startled her.

Looking down from her window, she saw the panel truck pulling into the drive, slowing to a crawl to pull in on the far side of the house. The truck rocked to a halt, its open sides letting the early sun glint off the metal crate racks. Mama was driving,

Agnes saw as the windshield angled into the shade of the house and she could see through it.

Daddy opened the passenger door and turned sideways on the seat, lifting his knees to swivel carefully around. He was only wearing one of his boots now. His right foot was bandaged halfway up his calf with something thick and stiff. He pulled crutches from behind the seat and slid out, standing on his left foot.

Agnes stared, her breath quick and light. He was all right. He looked all right. He was clumsy with the crutches. Mama came around the front of the truck and Agnes could hear her voice, but not what she was saying. Then she gestured toward the house and Daddy shook his head, pointing the other direction—toward the milk house.

Agnes froze. They would see the wagon loaded with crates and Mary leading the horses around by herself—and Daddy would be furious. He never let Mary handle the horses alone, especially not Franklin. Agnes whirled away from the window and ran.

CHAPTER THIRTEEN

Racing downstairs, Agnes nearly fell, then righted herself as she started down the long hall. She was out the door and across the barnyard before Mama came into sight, walking along the side of the house, coming slowly, as though she was tired. She waved wearily at Agnes and turned toward the back door. "Just let me wash my face and I'll be out to help," she called.

"Agnes!" Daddy called as he came around the corner. "Is everything all right?"

Agnes glanced out the gate toward the barn and nearly cried out. Mary was standing on the footrest and she was shaking the reins. Charles had opened the front gate and was standing by it. Agnes glanced back at Daddy. In two more awkward, swinging lurches, he was beside her, past the hedge, and he could see what she was seeing.

"What in blue blazes do you think you are doing?" Daddy shouted, and Agnes could only watch as he swung clumsily along on his crutches, crossing the barnyard, bearing down on Mary with an angry scowl on his face.

"We were just waiting for . . . Agnes was going to drive, really," Mary blurted out. "I was just turning the wagon around so we could hurry."

Agnes heard the back door open and saw her mother come down the porch steps. She sighed heavily without saying anything and they trailed Daddy across the barnyard.

"Is he going to be all right?" Agnes asked as they went.

"They say he will be fine," Mama told her. "It'll take some time, though, for the bone to heal."

"I was scared," Agnes said.

"I was, too," Mama said, reaching out to tug Agnes's hair. "Everything looks all right. Did you have any . . . " Mama took a half step, looking up to see the wagon for the first time. Daddy was standing beside it, saying something in a low, terse voice to Mary. Agnes looked at her. Her proud smile had vanished and she was ducking her head, looking upset.

"Delivering?" Daddy was demanding. "You were delivering?"

"We did the route last night," Agnes heard herself calling as she hurried toward them, Mama just behind her.

Daddy turned to look at her. "You what?"

"We delivered," Agnes said again, walking closer.

She heard her mother make a little sound of dismay, but didn't turn to look at her.

"You—" Daddy began, looking incredulous.

"We milked and bottled and delivered and made dinner and everything," Charles said. "I made dinner, that is. By myself."

Daddy was shaking his head. "You took the wagon to town? And just stacked the crates loose like this?"

Agnes could hear the disapproval in his voice. He glowered at Mary and she ducked her head again. She looked so upset that Agnes felt herself getting angry.

"We worked really hard," she said, a little too loudly.

Daddy took a deep breath. "You may have worked hard, but you didn't work smart. Agnes, what if something happened? What if—"

"It did," she interrupted. "The horses ran away. All the way down Main Street practically."

"But she stopped them," Charles put in. "Nothing got broken or anything." He finished his sentence, then caught himself, looking stricken. "Well, I broke two bottles."

Daddy's face tensed as he noticed the bandage on Charles's hand. "How bad are you hurt?"

Charles held out his hand. "Not bad at all, Daddy. The lady just bandaged me up because she wanted to help."

"What lady?" Daddy exploded. "Strangers had to help you out?" Daddy swung around to face Agnes. "I am so disappointed in you. I thought you had better sense."

Agnes stared into his eyes. He looked stern and tired and furious. Everything she had worried about was coming true. He was upset about them delivering, he was angry about the runaway . . . and it wasn't fair.

Agnes felt all her worry hardening into something else. "I have no sense? Like Ralph?" she said, without knowing she was going to say anything.

"What do you mean by that, young lady?" Daddy demanded.

"I spent the whole time worrying about what you would get upset about," Agnes heard herself saying. "I knew it would be something. Maybe that's why Ralph left. Maybe he got tired of working and never getting thanked." She pressed her lips together, watching his face.

Daddy was so surprised at her outburst that he just stared at her.

"Mary and Charles worked like the dickens and so did I," Agnes added, her anger boiling over into more words that she couldn't hold back. "If we didn't do everything right, I'm sorry. But we tried."

"Agnes helped Dilly have her calf, too," Charles put in.

"And we didn't have to dump any milk at all,"

Mary said very quietly. "Mama said to dump the milk but we didn't because Agnes thought of using the wagon."

Daddy glanced at Mama and Agnes followed his gaze. Mama was staring at him, her eyes cloudy and soft. "Maybe dairying is a lot like cleaning up an old woodpile," she said very clearly.

"Alice, what are you talking about?" Daddy almost shouted.

Mama smiled at him. "Sometimes things just go wrong. It doesn't mean anyone is to blame."

Daddy shook his head, swaying awkwardly on the crutches. "I've already said I was a fool to be walking around in a barnyard with holes in my boots. I admitted it, didn't I?" His voice was tight and low.

Mama touched his hand. "Why don't you just thank your children for taking care of the dairy while we were gone."

Daddy pulled in a deep breath and met Agnes's eyes. She could see him struggling to find words he could live with, that his pride and stubbornness would allow him to say.

"Thank you," he said finally. "I'm glad everything worked out all right."

"I'll make some breakfast," Mama said.

"Aggie already made pancakes for us," Mary said, her eyes flickering back and forth between Mama and Daddy.

"Then I'll just make something quick for your father and me," she said, then paused. "I'll back the truck around first," she added. "The kids can load the milk crates while you eat, then I'll drive the route with them."

Daddy was shaking his head, rubbing at his unshaven chin with one hand. Finally, he chuckled, then smiled. "Guess the customers were all surprised to see an old hay wagon and kids carrying the crates."

"They were probably just happy to see their milk arrive for the evening," Mama said.

Daddy leaned on the crutches and lifted one hand to push his hair back from his forehead. "It looks like I am out of a job here," he said gruffly. "Milk's bottled, you're going to drive the truck."

"For a while anyway, like Doc Lammee said," Mama told him. Then she looked at Agnes. "I was wondering how I would manage without Ralph. Now I know and that's one less worry, Agnes. Thank you all," she said, waiting for Daddy to get himself turned around on the crutches. "I am very proud of all three of you."

Watching her parents start back toward the house, Agnes wondered if what she'd said was true—that Ralph had left because Daddy was so hard on him. She would ask him—if she ever saw him again. And if she got the chance, she would apologize to him for being angry at him for so long, instead of just missing him and hoping he was all right.

"Agnes?"

She looked up. Mama was leaning out the back door.

"I'll bring the truck around now. Hold the horses."

"I will, Mama," Agnes yelled, and she started toward the wagon. Mary was smiling at her and Charles had his usual serious expression.

"Daddy was really proud of us, wasn't he," he said.

Agnes nodded. "He really was."

Charles nodded, as if something had been settled. The sputtering sound of the truck motor came from the other side of the house, and Agnes walked around and got a firm grip on the horses' reins. "Daddy's going to be all right," she said to Blaze. Then she smiled. It was true. Everything was going to be all right. They would manage just fine.

Friday, June 9, 1933
A sunny day after last night's rain.

Hiding out here by the haystack again . . . I won't be able to stay very long, though. Mama and Daddy went to town and I am supposed to be cleaning the horses' stall. Doctor Lammee is going to check Daddy's foot today. Daddy says he wants to walk without the crutches, but Mama says he will have to do whatever he is told and that's that. He is grumpy the last couple days, but I don't blame him. He can't do much and he is bored from sitting around the house all day for so long.

I haven't had a single chance to write till now. Mama says it could be another three weeks or so before Daddy can do his usual work. But we are managing without him, though it isn't easy. Mary and Charles are exhausted from all the work and so am I, but we have gotten quicker and better and Mama says we are a great team. She is so tired every night, but she wakes up smiling like she always has. Everything is going to be okay. Now, I am not going to write another word about work and worry because that's all I do and I am tired of it!!

The best thing is that we got a letter from Ralph yesterday. He is in Ohio! No one ever thought he would go so far, but he says he has a job at a dairy there and has promised Mama that he will send part of his pay home as soon as he can. I guess he had to use his first two checks to get set up in a boardinghouse and buy some work clothes and things like that. Daddy is angry, but he is also relieved just to know that Ralph is all right, I can tell. Mama cried reading the letter and had an answer written so fast she was folding it up before the ink was dry.

Ralph's letter said his boss told him he was the best milker he had ever seen and that someone sure taught him right. That made Daddy smile—and it made me wonder again. Maybe Ralph did leave because he was fed up with never hearing Daddy say anything nice about his work. I wrote Ralph back, too, and mailed it yesterday. I asked him if he was ever going to come home. I hope he will. I miss him a lot now that I am not so mad at him. Charles wrote him, too, his letters all big and crooked, and I know Ralph will love to see it. Mary wouldn't write her own letter, but she added a few lines to Charles's.

Coyotes got into the chickens last night and killed a hen. The only good thing about it is that now Daddy is talking about getting a puppy. He says we need a barnyard dog. Charles is beside himself, and it turns out that Mr. Thomas has a fine litter of coonhounds almost ready to wean. Daddy never hunts, but coon dogs make good barnyard dogs, Mr. Thomas says. Mrs. Otto is thinking about getting one, too, I think. I am excited. I love puppies and have wanted one for a whole year.

I saw Dilly out to pasture again this morning with her new heifer. It's a beautiful, perfect little yellow Guernsey. I want to go see Mrs. Otto when I can get the time. Maybe tomorrow between milkings. I told Mama and Daddy about Dilly, but then Mrs. Otto talked to them about it, too. Mama said she was proud of me, helping like that. I loved seeing the new baby. Mama says maybe I should be a veterinarian. I would LOVE that, I think. But she said it takes years of schooling and you have to go to college and study. So I guess I better pay attention to Mrs. Wright this year and get A's if I can.

I will write more later. I have to get back up to the house now. I hear the truck.

Sometimes one day can change a life forever

Different girls,
living in different periods of America's past
reveal their hearts' secrets in the pages
of their diaries. Each one faces a challenge
that will change her life forever.
Don't miss any of their stories:

#1 ❧ *Sarah Anne Hartford*
#2 ❧ *Emma Eileen Grove*
#3 ❧ *Anisett Lundberg*
#4 ❧ *Mary Alice Peale*
#5 ❧ *Willow Chase*
#6 ❧ *Ellen Elizabeth Hawkins*
#7 ❧ *Alexia Ellery Finsdale*
#8 ❧ *Evie Peach*
#9 ❧ *Celou Sudden Shout*
#10 ❧ *Summer MacCleary*
#11 ❧ *Agnes May Gleason*

JUN 22 1999